MW00874276

DEADLY LEGACY

Strong Women, Extraordinary Situations
Book Seven

Margaret Daley

Copyright

Deadly Legacy

Copyright © 2016 by Margaret Daley

The Inheritance Collection

A billionaire's bequest changes everything...

Billionaire Harold Hopewell traveled the world, encountering people and letting their stories touch him. In death, he is giving back, leaving an unusual will filled with life-altering bequests to the people he met along the way. Read the Inheritance Series, and let their stories touch you.

Check out all the books in
The Inheritance Collection at
http://theinheritanceseries.com/

Strong Women,
Extraordinary Situations Series

Layton, Felder, Bach & Moore
Attorneys-at-Law
58 East 42nd Street, Suite 1800
New York, New York 10016

Lacey St. John
670 David Ave.
New Orleans, LA 70117

Dear Mrs. St. John,

I am acting as the executor of the estate of Mr. Harold Hopewell, whose Last Will and Testament was entered into probate in the Surrogate's Court, New York County, State of New York. I write to inform you of certain assets bequeathed to you pursuant to Mr. Hopewell's Last Will and Testament, to wit:

Calvert Cove Bed and Breakfast in Calvert County in Maryland, the land it sits on, and all its content.

I have enclosed the deed to the property and an inventory of items in the house and on the grounds. As per our conversation, this is the ancestral house and acreage your family owned until twenty years ago when Mr. Hopewell bought it. He wanted to return the place to you with the added possessions specifically bought for the bed and breakfast.

Please do not hesitate to contact me with any questions.

Regards,
Frederick Bach, Esquire

ONE

Lacey St. John stared at the childhood residence she'd grown up in, now a thriving bed and breakfast, and fought the tears blurring her vision. This was her chance to turn her life around and provide a home for her son. Finally.

She blew out a long breath, facing the massive restored three-story Victorian dwelling. *It's mine after almost twenty years.*

Her eyes slid closed. Memories of the last day she'd lived in this house flooded her mind. Packing up what belongings that hadn't been sold to pay her father's debts. Wondering if she would ever be able to come back—the only home she'd known for twelve years. As her dad had driven away, she'd turned and watched the house fade from her view. All their remaining possessions had been packed in boxes and bags that had been crammed into every available space in their van.

"Mom!"

A tug on her arm grounded her in the present. She glanced at Shaun, his big brown eyes wide as he looked at her.

"We're gonna live here?" her eight-year-old son asked, doubt dominating his features. "It's *big*."

"That it is. When I lived here, there were a lot of great hiding places. My sister and I used to play hide and seek all the time."

"And it's ours now?"

Since her husband had died three years ago, she and Shaun had moved around a lot in New Orleans. Their last apartment had been in a dangerous neighborhood. Not a night went by that they didn't hear a siren or gunshots. "Honey, yes. Thanks to Harold Hopewell. He left us Calvert Cove

Bed and Breakfast."

"C'mon." He dragged her to the porch that ran the length of most of the front.

As she and Shaun mounted the steps, the carved and beveled glass door opened. A middle-aged woman with sandy blond hair in a tight bun and a bland expression on her face stood in the entrance. Lacey had called ahead to let the manager, Mrs. Bell, know they were coming. This lady must be her.

Lacey marched forward with her hand held out. "I'm Lacey St. John. And this is my son, Shaun. Are you Harriet Bell?"

The forty-something's gaze remained on Lacey. "Yes. I wasn't expecting you for another hour." She moved to the side to allow them inside.

Lacey dropped her arm without shaking the woman's hand. "How are the renovations coming?" Calvert Cove had been scheduled for an update before Mr. Hopewell died, and there were provisions for it to be completed while she took over ownership. It would allow her to become familiar with the bed and breakfast and the staff before guests returned in three weeks.

"One of the painters came down sick and won't be here today, but otherwise everything is progressing as it should." Mrs. Bell shut the front door after they entered. "I made sure the carriage house was readied first. I thought you would like to live there rather than in here."

For the time being, Lacey kept silent, but once she was settled and the renovations were completed, she intended to live in the main house, if not before then. Mrs. Bell probably wasn't aware of Lacey's previous association with Calvert Cove.

"I'd like to do a walkthrough after we unload the car."

"I can have my husband take care of unloading your car for you. I'll let him know and be right back."

As Mrs. Bell left the large foyer, a vision of Lacey sliding down the banister flitted across her mind. She smiled. She'd done it when no one was around because her mother used to freak out at the thought of a scraped knee. Growing up here, she'd had her share of mishaps, especially when she tried to scale the small cliff behind her house or to clamber down the rope on the boom at the carriage house. Now she knew better, but back then, she'd been lucky she'd only fallen a couple of times—with no broken bones.

Next to her, Shaun fidgeted. She grasped his shoulder as Mrs. Bell returned to the entry hall, which was almost bigger than their last apartment.

The manager gestured toward the wide staircase. "We can start on the third floor and work our way to the basement."

"Are there guest rooms in the basement?"

"Two. The Garden and Cliffside Suites along the rear. The rest of the basement is for storage and laundry."

"Where do you and your husband stay?"

"In the Cliffside Suite. It comes with the job." Mrs. Bell started up the stairs. On the midway landing, she went to the right then crossed the corridor to the steps that led to the third floor.

When Calvert Cove was first built in the

1870s, the top floor was where servants lived. It had rarely been used when her family had lived in the house. "How many rooms are there?"

"Four. When Mr. Hopewell had this house converted to a bed and breakfast, certain walls were knocked out and the layout changed from the original house."

"How long ago was that?"

"Nineteen years ago this place became a bed and breakfast. I've been working in one capacity or another all that time. I started as a maid while Richard, my husband, arrived fifteen years ago as the Sous-Chef. Now he's the Chef de Cuisine, and we serve dinner opened to the public five days a week while breakfast is only for the guests."

For a moment, Lacey wondered if there would be a place she could fit in at the bed and breakfast. She now owned it, but with Mrs. Bell, she got the impression everything was running smoothly the way it was, so what could she do to improve things? Lacey only had one year of college when she'd met Jason, a talented musician, and was swept off her feet. They married, and she went with him as he played in a band and traveled all over the world. Then everything changed when she became pregnant with Shaun. They settled down in New Orleans where Jason could play, but he had wanderlust in his blood and had never been happy in one place for long.

"Your husband cooks?" Shaun asked as he passed them in the upstairs hallway and raced to the end to look out the big window. "Mom, I can see the water from here." He tapped on the glass. "Is that the carriage house?"

While Mrs. Bell, with her arms crossed and lips pinched, stopped at the nearest bedroom door, Lacey made her way to Shaun and leaned forward. "Yes, that's it."

"What's a carriage house?"

"A fancy name for a garage. Back when this house was built, they didn't have cars. They rode in carriages and on horses to get where they wanted to go."

"Why would we have to live in the garage? I thought you owned this house."

Lacey suppressed her smile and turned

toward Mrs. Bell. "My son has a point. Why would we want to, Mrs. Bell?"

Red suffused the older woman's cheeks. "Personally, I thought you would want to have privacy from the guests who come. The carriage house gives you that. We still have work to do on the rooms on the first, second, and third floors, and the house tends to be noisy. The only places in the main house ready now are the two suites in the basement." She bowed her head slightly. "Of course, you have the choice to stay anywhere on the property. But some of our rooms have been requested and reserved for some of the returning guests in the coming months. We have one couple that comes every year in the fall and stays in the Baltimore Oriole Suite."

"I'll take the other suite in the basement for now. I have three weeks to choose where we'll stay." She walked back to Mrs. Bell. "I'm not here to sit and do nothing. I intend to take an active role in running the bed and breakfast."

Mrs. Bell raised her cold, gray gaze to hers. "I'm at your service. Now this room," she opened the door and entered, "is called the Chesapeake Bay Suite because it has a good view of the water."

For a fleeting moment, Lacey shivered from a chill that swept through her.

* * *

Sheriff Ryan McNeil stepped out onto his deck to relish the warm April evening after a long day at work. At least he was home at a reasonable time today. Lately, he'd been tied up with a series of burglaries. He and his deputies had finally caught two guys this afternoon. Looking through the leafing white oaks along the back of his property, he glimpsed Chesapeake Bay. This was his haven, a home that had been in his family for over a hundred years.

At the railing, he drew in a deep breath of the flower-scented air, enjoying the quiet. He'd spent the whole afternoon interviewing one of the two burglars, only to discover they were part of a larger ring. He'd deal with that tomorrow. For now, he needed to take Mick for a walk after being cooped up all day in the house.

He went inside, called his mutt, and picked up his leash. Mick bounded into the kitchen, yelping. His dog was a combination of several big breeds with brown and black coloring. Mick never met a stranger. He loved people, sometimes getting carried away with his greetings. Ryan was working on that with Mick, but he had been for a couple of years.

They headed out the front door and down the long bricked walk to the road. "Which way do you want to go, Mick?"

His dog sniffed the air, looked up and down the street, and then went left. This was a daily ritual between them, but usually he chose right. What did he smell that made him pick this route?

A minute later, Ryan discovered why he wanted to go this way. After passing the drive to the Calvert Cove Bed and Breakfast, Mick tugged him toward a row of three-foot-high scrubs along the street, part of the beautifully landscaped property.

Ryan caught sight of something red among the greenery. He moved closer.

Mick stuck his head into the middle bush, his tail wagging.

"What did you find?" Ryan came nearer.

A young boy shot up through the foliage and glanced at the house behind him. When he returned his attention to Ryan, the child said, "I'm hiding."

"You are? Why?"

"I told Mom she wouldn't be able to find me. She used to play hide-n-seek all the time here when she was a little girl."

"How long have you been hiding?" Ryan scanned the front of the bed and breakfast, not realizing the place was taking guests. He thought the renovation would last for several more weeks.

The boy shrugged. "A *long* time."

Which in child speak could be anywhere from five minutes to five hours. Ryan smiled. He used to play all kinds of games outside as a kid with others in the neighborhood. He was trying to remember the family who lived here before the place was sold and turned into a bed and breakfast. The Randalls? Yes, that was it. There were two girls, but he didn't remember much else.

"I'm Ryan. I live next door." He pointed toward the large white, colonial-styled house peeking through the trees.

"Are you a policeman?"

Ryan glanced at his tan uniform. "Yep, and this is Mick."

The child held out his hand for the dog to smell before he petted him. "I wish I had a dog."

"Where do you live?"

The kid pointed to the house.

"When you're not on vacation?"

"I'm not on vacation. Mom says I have to start school here on Monday. Yuck." The boy puckered his lips as if he'd had too many lemons.

Was his mother another live-in employee? He was usually familiar with the people who worked at the bed and breakfast. He didn't realize there would be a new person. Richard and Harriet Bell were the only ones who lived on the property. He hadn't talked to them in a week with his crazy long hours, but maybe he should. The Calvert Cove Bed and

Breakfast was renowned in this region and had brought in a lot of tourists. He liked to stay on top of what was going on there.

"Shaun! Where are you? The game is over."

The child whirled around. "I've gotta go."

Before Ryan could say anything, the boy shot out of the shrubbery and raced across the yard. The woman spied him plowing his way through a rose garden, mindless of the flowers he was trying to dodge and not always succeeding. Even from a distance Ryan saw the lady wince as Shaun leaped over the last bush and fell short.

"What do you think, Mick? Should we introduce ourselves?"

His dog barked once as Shaun picked himself up from the ground and continued forward, limping slightly.

"Okay, since she and her son will be living here." Ryan would forgo charging through the row of scrubs. Instead he took the long way back to the driveway and strolled toward the porch.

While he covered the distance to the woman with long blond hair pulled into a ponytail, he overheard her conversation with her son. She wasn't too pleased that Shaun had hidden outside. Obviously she'd spent the last half hour searching the house.

"Mom, you didn't tell me I couldn't go outside."

"You need to wash up. Dinner will be ready soon."

Shaun hung his head and shuffled toward the front door while the woman kept her blue gaze fixed on Ryan as he approached her.

"I'm Sheriff Ryan McNeil. I live next door."

She shook his hand. "I'm Lacey St. John, the new owner of this bed and breakfast."

"Ah, that explains why your son said he lives here."

"Yes, we arrived earlier today."

"Welcome to the area. This part of the peninsula is usually quiet."

"That's good." She tilted her head to

the side. "How long have you lived here?"

"All my life, thirty-five years."

"Ah, that's why your name sounds familiar. I lived here until I was twelve. I was Lacey Randall back then. My older sister had a crush on you."

"Your sister is—Laura?"

"Yes, she was two years older than me and was boy crazy back then. Now she's happily married and living in Colorado."

"I'm glad to hear that. How did you end up back here?"

"Mr. Hopewell bequeathed the bed and breakfast to me in his will. It came out of the blue, but I thank God every day he did. Only a couple of days earlier there had been a murder in my apartment building in New Orleans."

"We haven't had a murder in this county for a couple of years, and I hope to keep it that way."

Lacey glanced over her shoulder at the front door. "I know this is last minute, but if you haven't had dinner, come join us. From what I saw in the kitchen, Richard prepared enough food to feed us and then some. I'd love to hear how this area has changed since I moved away. I always had fond memories of living here."

"Since my cooking is lousy, I'm not going to pass up that offer. I'll take Mick home then come back."

"Great. I'll let Richard know we're having another guest for dinner."

As Ryan cut across their yards, avoiding any flowerbeds, out of the corner of his eye, he caught a movement in the shadows of dusk. He stopped and stared at the rear of the carriage house. He walked closer. He didn't see anyone, but then Mick started growling.

TWO

A short, stocky figure, dressed in black, shot out of a crevice of darkness at the far end of the carriage house and ran toward the small cliff at the back of the property.

Ryan dropped his dog's leash. "Stay, Mick." He charged across the yard after the suspicious man who had at least a fifty-yard head start.

The runner changed directions and plunged into the thick vegetation between his place and the acreage owned by the bed and breakfast. By the time Ryan chased him through the wooded area and emerged a few feet from the twelve-foot drop-off, the man had hopped into a motorboat, started its engine, and drove in the direction of Annapolis. The deep shoe prints near the water's edge indicated that the intruder must have jumped from where he had been and landed in the small sandy cove.

The only thing Ryan glimpsed was the all-white boat with its name, *Sea Princess*, printed in black across the aft. The smaller lettering underneath was too hard to read. As he watched it speeding away, he dug his cell phone out of his pants pocket and called the station.

When Deputy Blake Simmons answered, Ryan identified himself. "A man was hanging around the bed and breakfast and ran when I headed toward him. He got away in a boat about twenty feet long called the *Sea Princess*. He was going toward Annapolis. Check into it. Something was fishy about him, no pun intended."

"I will. Do you think he could be part of the burglary gang?"

"Possibly casing the house, although I don't think the two we have in custody have used a boat as a getaway vehicle, but maybe they're changing things up since we caught a couple of them today."

Ryan made his way down the cliff, used his phone to take a photo of the shoe print in the sand, then hiked back to Mick and resumed his trek to his house. On his return to the bed and breakfast, he studied the area where he caught sight of the guy. Again he took pictures of what appeared to be footprints of tennis shoes similar to the ones at the small cove. Why had the stranger been hanging around the carriage house? There were two suites in the small building, all signs of its original purpose gone. He tried the door. Locked. To be on the safe side, he intended to check inside later.

* * *

"He's here!" Shaun yelled from the foyer.

Lacey cringed. She was glad she wasn't in the same room as Mrs. Bell, who no doubt disapproved of screaming and kids. As she walked toward the entrance hall,

Lacey realized she only had three weeks to teach her son to be quiet as a mouse. Maybe the carriage house was the best place for them to live. She would check it out. She remembered it as a garage with rooms where items no longer wanted by her parents were stored as well as an empty attic running the length of the building where hay used to be stored in the late nineteenth and early twentieth centuries.

She entered the reception area.

"Can I come over and see Mick?" Shaun asked the sheriff. "I've wanted a dog *forever*. We could never have one in New Orleans. But now we have a great big yard for one."

Ryan glanced up at her, his dark eyes twinkling. "Sure you can come visit Mick, but only if your mom says it's okay."

Shaun whirled around toward her. "Did ya hear? I can play with Mick until you get me my own dog."

"Hold it right there. We haven't talked about that yet. We aren't going to rush into anything. Hon, you have to remember in a few weeks there will be guests here all the time, and we can't just do what we want."

"I thought we owned the house. Why can't we?"

"This isn't only a home but a place of business." Tonight she would need to set up rules. If she didn't spell out exactly what he could and couldn't do, Shaun would go his merry way—like when he hid outside in the shrubs earlier because she hadn't made it clear only the first floor of the house was to be used for the game.

"But why—"

"Did you wash your hands?" she interrupted, hoping to take his mind off of getting a dog.

Shaun stared at them. "I did—I forgot to use soap."

"Go. Mrs. Bell said dinner is in ten minutes in the dining room."

While her son darted past her, Lacey moved forward. "I'm afraid Shaun is going to be at your house every day the minute he sees your car there. All the way here this morning, he talked about finally getting a dog. Now I'm not so sure." She glanced from side to side and lowered her voice. "Mrs. Bell doesn't seem the kind of person who would like a dog underfoot."

Ryan chuckled. "She comes across prim and proper, but she loves Mick. Occasionally, when I can't make it home at night, she'll go over to my house, walk him, and feed him for me."

"So she isn't really prim and proper." She would have used the words, cranky and cold.

"Well, when it comes to running this place, she is serious and focused. When she became manager a few years back, she was elated. She didn't want to let Mr. Hopewell down." Ryan cleared his throat. "I need to check out the carriage house, preferably before dinner."

"Why? Is something wrong?"

"A while ago, I caught a man lurking around it, and then when he saw me, he ran. We've had a burglary ring working this area."

"And you think the man was casing this place?" She headed in the direction of the kitchen where the Bells were. "There's a set of keys in the office off the kitchen. I'll grab the ones to the two suites at the carriage house while you explain about the man to Mr. and Mrs. Bell."

Lacey retrieved the key and paused to take in the neat and orderly office. She had to admit she was intimidated by Mrs. Bell and couldn't see the woman any other way than stiff as a board with eyes that could freeze her. That image in her thoughts caused laughter to bubble to the surface as she reentered the kitchen.

"Mrs. Bell, the sheriff and I are going out to look at the carriage house to see the two suites."

"Harriet, we won't be long. I don't think he broke in, but I want to make sure." Ryan gave the manager a smile.

And the woman grinned back.

That was the first time Lacey had seen that expression on her face.

Shaun raced into the room. "Wait for me! Where are we going?"

Lacey looked at Ryan, and he answered, "I understand the suites in the carriage house have been renovated, and your mother's going to give me a quick tour before dinner."

"I'm coming, too." Shaun planted himself between Lacey and Ryan.

"As long as you don't touch anything."

Her son opened his mouth to say something.

Lacey hurried to finish. "Or you can stay here and help Mrs. Bell put dinner on the table."

Shaun's eyes grew round, his eyebrows shooting up. "I won't touch a thing," he said in a sober voice.

Lacey pressed her lips together. She'd found something that might keep her son's "enthusiasm" contained. The old saying, "a bull in a china shop," definitely fit Shaun. He was growing so fast, his mind wasn't keeping up with his long legs and arms.

At the carriage house, she handed the keys to Ryan, who opened the main door into a short hallway with a suite on each side. They entered the one on the right first, exposing a large sitting area, bedroom, and bathroom. A big bay window overlooked the front of the property. While

Ryan, with Shaun's help, went through the suite, she peered outside toward Ryan's three-story white-bricked Colonial-styled house. Its clean, straight lines seemed to fit what she'd seen of its owner. They all toured the second set of rooms, similar to the first one except that its bay window afforded glimpses of the water through the trees along the back of the yard. When they finished, she looked at Ryan and mouthed the word, "Anything?"

Ryan shook his head. "I don't know about you, Shaun, but Richard is a terrific chef. My mouth is watering just thinking about what he'll be serving us."

"What?" Shaun asked as they traipsed to the main house.

"Beef Wellington." Ryan opened the back door to the kitchen and allowed Lacey to go in first.

"Great! I like beef, especially a hamburger." Shaun dashed through the kitchen for the entrance into the dining room.

"It's a little more than…" Ryan chuckled. "I guess he doesn't care."

"He might when he sees it. I'm praying he doesn't show his disappointment. He isn't into fancy dishes." Before joining Shaun, Lacey stopped Ryan. "Did you see anything that concerned you at the carriage house?"

"No, but I'll walk around it again on my way home tonight."

Ryan held a chair out for Lacey and then scooted it in for her. He took the seat across from her. "Richard, the Beef Wellington looks delicious. I know this is one of your signature dishes, but I've never had it."

The chef grinned. "I always love hearing that. I thought in honor of our new owner's arrival, I'd prepare it for dinner." He raised his water glass. "To Mrs. St. John and the young master." Richard glanced at Shaun.

Her son turned beet red.

"I appreciate the special dinner, Mr. Bell." Lacey took the platter he handed her with the Beef Wellington in the center and the potatoes and wilted greens circling the main dish.

"Richard, please."

Lacey scooped the food onto her plate then onto Shaun's. "What I've seen of the renovations looks great. The first floor shouldn't take too much longer. When does the contractor think it will be done?"

"The first floor in a couple of days. He had a painter sick today. Tom Avant called and told me a while ago that he had to let that man go. It seems he isn't sick after all but left town. Until he hires another one, the work will progress more slowly." Mrs. Bell passed the platter to Ryan.

"Will that delay our reopening?" There was so much Lacey needed to learn. "I've painted before and could pitch in if needed."

"Nonsense. Everything is being taken care of." Mrs. Bell cut her meat and took a bite.

Lacey gripped her fork. "I realize you're very efficient, Mrs. Bell, but I'm willing to help where needed."

"That's not your job."

Lacey gritted her teeth to keep from saying something she would regret. Mrs. Bell had been running the bed and breakfast for years and didn't want anyone treading on her territory, but Lacey couldn't sit and do nothing. She'd always worked hard to support herself and Shaun. She would quickly go stir-crazy if she didn't.

"I like this a lot, Richard. Can you put the meat between two pieces of bread like a hamburger?"

Lacey nearly choked on the sip of tea she swallowed at the exact time her son spoke. Mrs. Bell's face turned redder than Shaun's had a few minutes earlier.

"Little kids shouldn't call him Richard." The manager shot to her feet. "Excuse me. I forgot the butter."

"But, honey, we don't need..." Her husband's voice faded into silence as his wife disappeared into the kitchen.

Shaun's eyes glistened with unshed tears. He stared at the empty seat then at Lacey. "I thought he said I could."

Richard smiled. "I did. It's okay, if your mother agrees."

"We'll talk about it later. My son is right. This is delicious."

Shaun lowered his head and stared at

his lap.

Silence fell over the table. Thick. Stifling.

Richard rose. "I'm going to check on Harriet. She may need help carrying the butter in here." He winked at Shaun and grasped the boy's shoulder briefly as he passed him on the way to the kitchen.

Ryan's gaze caught Lacey's for a few seconds before he said, "Shaun, you mentioned something about starting school on Monday. What grade are you in?"

* * *

In the living area of the Garden Suite, Ryan stood at the picture window that spanned the length of one wall while Lacey said good night to her son. In the distance, a few twinkling lights across the bay sprinkled the darkness. The backyard gardens, especially the rose bushes, would dominate Lacey's view during the daytime. In the past when the bed and breakfast wasn't full, he'd sat on the patio with Harriet and Richard as the sun went down.

But lately, since the renovations started, that had been rare. The Bells had worked hard to make this place one of the best along the Eastern Seaboard.

When the couple returned to the dining room table without the plate of butter, the tension had eased when Richard regaled them with stories of some of his earlier disastrous attempts at cooking. He even managed to get a smile from Shaun toward the end.

"I can't wait to have my tea tomorrow morning on the patio. Laura, my sister, and I used to do that when the weather was nice. We felt so grown up."

Ryan rotated slowly toward Lacey who crossed the room and stopped next to him. A vanilla scent teased his senses. Upstairs during dinner, it had competed with aromas from the food, but now it stood out, centering his full attention on the pretty woman before him.

"Is Shaun okay now?"

"Better because Richard was great at putting him at ease. Is Mrs. Bell always like she was?"

"No, but I imagine she's concerned. When she heard Mr. Hopewell died, she took his death real hard. Change is hard for Harriet."

"It's for me, too, but this should be a good move for us, even with her attitude. We didn't live in a safe neighborhood. I'd been trying to save money to move somewhere else, but my late husband had a lot of debt that had to be repaid."

"I'm sorry. How long ago did he pass away?"

"Three years but I finally managed to pay everything off a couple of months ago, and then Mr. Hopewell left me this bed and breakfast. I was sure things were starting to look up for Shaun and me. I need this to work out."

"Don't let Harriet get to you."

"I won't, but I realize I should have a word with her. I'm not looking forward to that meeting. I don't want her to leave here, but neither do I want to walk around afraid to say or do anything. Nor do I want that for Shaun. He was so excited to have a house to live in. We've been living in a tiny, one-bedroom apartment."

"Is your sister one of the owners, too?" He could remember Laura's attempt to get his attention while growing up—like making him cookies. As though he wouldn't be able to tell that there had been more salt than sugar in them.

"No, she and her husband have a good life in Colorado. She asked me to come and stay with them when they moved into their big house six months ago, but they don't have any children, and she's never wanted any. I didn't think that would be a good fit for Shaun and me." One corner of her mouth quirked. "By then, I could see daylight at the end of the tunnel."

"You said you wanted to talk to me about something."

Her forehead crinkled, and worry filled her beautiful crystalline blue eyes. "Yes. With that guy lurking around and burglars in the area, I've been thinking about what I should do. When guests start coming in a few weeks, I want this house safe for them."

"First, I hope to have caught the rest of

the burglary ring by then. We have two of them in custody. I'm not familiar with the security system, but I can take a look and make suggestions to upgrade if needed. The use of cameras might be something you could look into."

She released a long breath, some of her concern fading from her expression. "Thank you. I was hoping you would volunteer. All I know about security is locks on the doors and windows."

"That's a start, and yes, I'll help you. I'd rather prevent a crime than have to solve it. I'll check into it before the bed and breakfast reopens."

"I'm glad you live next door. When I was a little girl, I loved living here. I have such fond memories of this place."

"That's why I chose to return home. We're near Washington D.C., but most of the time it seems to be hundreds of miles away."

"Did you live in Washington?"

A lifetime ago. One he wanted to forget. "Yes, for seven years. I worked for the FBI. I was recruited right out of college. When my mother decided to move to Florida to be near her sister, I thought I would live here and commute. Have the peace and quiet this place offers and still do my job working in a counter terrorism group."

"What changed your mind?"

"I have my doctorate in psychology with an emphasis on criminal behavior. I discovered I needed a balance in my life. Being sheriff allows me to still serve the community, but it also gives me that balance. My job isn't totally dealing with criminals dedicated to hurting people and destroying this country."

"I'm glad. I can only imagine what studying criminal behavior can do to a person. In my neighborhood in New Orleans, I saw my share of felons."

He wanted to ask her more about her life before coming here to live, but he noticed a slump to her shoulders and a tiredness in her eyes. "I'd better go. Mick will be wondering why I got to have all the fun while he stayed home." He walked to the door, put his hand on the knob, and glanced back. "I hope Shaun will come over and play with Mick. He'd love the attention."

"Who? Shaun or Mick?"

He stepped into the hallway. "Both. I'm going out by the patio. Make sure the outside door is locked behind me."

She followed him, and when he left the house, he heard the click as the lock was turned.

Using a small pocket flashlight, he decided to circle the carriage house on his way home. Something didn't feel right, but nothing he saw alerted him to what it could be.

While he strolled toward his back door, his cell phone rang. Calls late at night were never a good thing. "Sheriff McNeil here."

"The *Sea Princess* was stolen, but it's been found. Someone torched it."

THREE

Shaun rushed into the office off the kitchen. "I'm going to Ryan's to play with Mick. He just came home."

Lacey looked up from going through the books for the bed and breakfast. "You haven't even told me how your first day at school went."

"Great. I met some kids who live near here. The bus let Mark off right in front of his house, only three away from here." He whirled around and raced out of the room before Lacey could tell him to slow down.

Not a second later, she heard a crash. Oh, no. Not again. She shoved herself to her feet and made her way into the kitchen. A tray with a plastic pitcher and glasses littered the floor between Mrs. Bell and her. Shaun stood frozen a few feet away.

"I'm sorry. I'm sorry." He crouched and began picking up the items.

Mrs. Bell's expression smoldered as she watched Shaun clean up the mess he caused. Surprisingly she remained quiet, but the narrow-eyed look on her face spoke volumes of what was going through the woman's mind, forcing Lacey to acknowledge it was time to have that conversation with Mrs. Bell. The past couple of days, there had been several encounters between the manager and her son, and each time Mrs. Bell's anger festered even deeper.

Lacey tried to ignore Mrs. Bell's glare, but it bored into her. "Shaun, no running in the house. Next time you won't get to go see Mick. This is your last warning."

"It's about time," Mrs. Bell mumbled and marched to the sink to wash the pitcher and glasses.

"I can dry them." Shaun grabbed the

towel.

"No. I'll take care of it. I told the workers I would bring them iced tea, and that is what I'm going to do."

"You can leave, Shaun." Lacey covered the distance between her and Mrs. Bell and picked up the towel her son laid on the counter by the sink. "Mrs. Bell, I'll take the drinks to the guys. My eyes are about to cross looking over the accounting ledger. I could use the break."

The woman continued to wash out the glasses and place them on the side of the sink away from Lacey.

She took calming breaths and moved in front of the wet dishes. "I'm sorry—"

"This is the third time since he came that we've had mishaps. When guests are here, that kind of behavior can't be tolerated. Most come to get away from the big city and have a peaceful vacation."

"I realize that, and I'll take care of Shaun. This is all new and exciting to him. He'll settle down." Since coming to the Calvert Cove B and B, her son had been different, as though he was embracing being a boy and having fun. He'd been so serious and solemn in the apartment.

As they finished cleaning the dishes, Lacey poured iced tea into the pitcher then slowly carried the tray upstairs to the second floor. The contractor stood in the hall at the end with a worker she hadn't met yet. She walked halfway down the corridor and put the drinks on a table. Then she continued toward Tom Avant.

"I'm going to leave the glasses and iced tea on the table. The workers can help themselves when they want something to drink." Lacey shifted her gaze to the unfamiliar man next to her. "I'm Lacey St. John, the owner. You must be the new painter."

"Yes, I'm Trey Dawson. I just arrived. Tom's giving me instructions on where to start."

"Thanks for being able to fill in the next few weeks."

As the tall man dressed in white coveralls left and took the stairs to the third story, Lacey asked, "How much longer until that floor is finished?"

"Maybe by late tomorrow or the day after. I've heard good things about Dawson. He came highly recommended. We were lucky to get him between jobs."

"Is he from around here?"

"Not too far away. Alexandria."

"That's good to hear. I've been impressed with the work so far. If you need me for anything, you've got my cell phone number." And she had Tom's.

As Lacey headed downstairs, she paused in the entrance to the Greene Suite, named after the first owner of the house, a distant relative in her mother's family. Mrs. Bell hadn't been too happy with her this morning when Lacey had let the contractor know that she would be taking over and had final say on the work.

Mrs. Bell did a good job running the bed and breakfast, but her sense of style was on the drab side. Lacey had learned a lot being the receptionist at a design firm. The dull crocodile green had to go. The addition of more accent colors in a few of the suites would brighten up the rooms. Lacey wanted the guests to leave here with an upbeat attitude.

There was nothing she could do but have the new painter redo the Greene Suite totally, and she still hadn't talked to Mrs. Bell about that or about Shaun. She didn't want to lose her as the manager, but Shaun was here to stay, and she wouldn't have her child intimidated by the woman.

When she reentered the kitchen, she kept going. She'd been cooped up all day in the office, familiarizing herself with how the bed and breakfast was run. She needed fresh air. Then maybe she would tackle the conversation with Mrs. Bell. When she left by the back door, she ran into Gus Kent, the main gardener who came three times a week, and his assistant, Paul Moore, tending to the rose beds that surrounded the carriage house on three sides.

She paused next to Gus. "I can't wait until these are all fully in bloom. I love roses."

He beamed. "Calvert Cove is getting quite a reputation for its gardens, especially the roses."

"And from what I understand, you're

the reason." Lacey spied Shaun outside with Mick, throwing a ball for the dog to fetch.

She made her way to Shaun. "Are you all right?"

"I didn't mean to run into her." He lobbed the red ball into the air, and Mick raced after it.

"I know, but you can't hurry through the house. You never did in the apartment."

"Mom, that place was tiny."

"And you were excited to see Mick."

"Ryan, too."

"Ryan?"

"He told me to call him that."

"Where is he?"

"He had a phone call, but he lets me come out here without him. Mick is well behaved. He won't run away."

The sound of Ryan's back door opening drew her focus. Her heartbeat picked up as the six-and-a-half-foot man with short black hair sauntered toward them. His dark brown eyes zeroed in on her, and her breath caught in her throat. Commanding.

Compelling. Then he grinned at her, his whole face lighting up. She wasn't sure what she liked the best about him—his eyes or smile.

For a few seconds, her knees went weak, and she had to toughen her resolve not to be enticed by him. Jason, her deceased husband, had attracted her the first moment she saw him. She never looked beyond his handsome features and charismatic pull. She didn't see the self-centeredness that turned their marriage quickly into one trial after another. She'd given up her dream to finish college to follow him from one gig to the next. His music had once captured her attention, but back then, she'd been young and starry-eyed. Not anymore.

"I didn't expect to see you. I've been so busy the past few days with the burglary gang and trying to track down the guy who was lurking around your carriage house, I haven't had time to come over and see how everything's going."

She glanced at her son, running and falling down to play-wrestle with the big dog. "Has Shaun been bugging you a lot about Mick?"

"No, he's been helping me. I was going to walk back with him yesterday evening until I received a call about another burglary five miles from here. I had to leave right away and grab dinner at a fast food restaurant on the way to the crime scene."

"Are you always this busy?"

"Thankfully, I'm not. Like I said the other day, this area is usually quiet. I'd hoped by now to have some positive information about your lurker. The getaway boat was found in shallow water, on fire. Not much left to process for fingerprints. The few we found were the owner's." He moved closer and lowered his husky voice. "I haven't forgotten about checking your security. If you don't mind, I can take a look tonight."

"Not at all." His presence, so close, caused flutters in her stomach. "I've been thinking. Do you know anyone who has a young dog for sale? Maybe not as big as Mick. Shaun wants a dog. I've been putting him off, especially because Mrs. Bell has her own vision of how the bed and breakfast should be, and I don't think that includes a pet other than a goldfish."

Shaun skidded to an abrupt halt inches from her. "Can I have one?"

"I guess there's nothing wrong with your hearing. I think goldfish would be great in a pond out in the garden. You could be in charge of taking care of them, and our guests will enjoy them." She wondered if the gardener could put in a pond.

"Mom, you were talking about a dog. Can I have one? I'd keep him out of Mrs. Bell's way. I promise."

The eager look on Shaun's face urged her to say yes, but then she remembered what happened earlier in the kitchen. She needed Mr. and Mrs. Bell. She'd never be able to run a bed and breakfast by herself. She had no experience and no—why did it have to be all or nothing? In the office where she worked, she had been the go-to person for a compromise. Surely she could come up with something for the Calvert

Cove B and B.

She captured Ryan's gaze. "Do you know of a dog like I described?"

"Possibly. Sid Carter's cocker spaniel had puppies two months ago. I think he still has a few left."

"A dog for me?" Wonder filled Shaun's voice.

"I'd like to look into it. But no guarantees. We have to find the right pet, because it'll be part of the bed and breakfast."

"I can take care of my pet. I can." Shaun hopped up and down, grinning from ear to ear. "It will never bother anyone."

"Would you two like to stay for dinner?" Ryan clasped her son's shoulder. "I ordered a pizza."

"Yes! My favorite." Shaun punched the air with his fist. "I'm in."

"How about you, Lacey?"

"Sure. We haven't had pizza in five days. I'll let Richard know we won't be there for dinner." She quickly made the call and ended up telling Mrs. Bell who answered the phone. Lacey was sure she'd heard relief in the manager's voice.

Ryan swept his arm across his body. "Then let me show you my house."

As though the white-bricked Colonial was his, Shaun ran with Mick toward the back door. "This is the best day ever."

Lacey walked with Ryan at a more sedate speed. "I'm glad he's putting the incident with Mrs. Bell behind him."

"What happened?"

"My son caused her to drop a tray of glasses and a pitcher. Thankfully, they were plastic and not filled. But Mrs. Bell wasn't pleased. Shaun apologized and picked up the dishes. She made it clear she wasn't pleased that a young boy was in the house. Do the guests ever bring children with them?"

"I've seen some over the years, but it's usually couples who frequent the bed and breakfast."

"Maybe that's it. She hasn't been around kids much."

Ryan opened the door for Lacey and followed her into a very modern kitchen in stark contrast to the outer appearance of his house.

"How old is this place?

"Another ten years, it'll be two hundred years old, but it's been updated several times through that period."

"I can see. You even have a microwave and convection oven."

"My mom loved to cook. Sadly, her son doesn't."

"That's a shame. I like to cook but haven't had much of an opportunity in the last few years. Richard is wonderful, but I hate to intrude on his kitchen."

Shaun and Mick appeared in the doorway to the dining room. "The pizza guy just pulled up. Let's eat." He twirled around and headed toward the front of the house.

"My son has made himself at home here."

"And my dog is trotting right after him."

* * *

Lacey turned her head toward Ryan. "You didn't have to walk us home. In case you don't know, we live next door."

The lights from the bed and breakfast softened her features, emphasizing her beautiful smile that gave her a glow. For a second, Ryan raised his hand to touch her lips until Mick barked, his tail wagging.

Ryan dropped his arm back in place and searched for Mick. His dog had his head buried in a hedge of azaleas, ready to bloom. "Mick, heel. Gus Kent has been babying these all year. He's determine to have the best display in the area this year."

Mick, on a leash that Shaun held, immediately returned to the boy's side.

"Gus does a great job with the gardens." Lacey moved closer and crouched to see what Mick was excited about. "It's too dark behind the hedge to see anything."

"I'll check tomorrow before I go to school."

"Not without me. Remember the rose bushes that you broke the branches off of last week. You need to go get ready for bed."

"Oh, man. I shouldn't have said anything about school." With slumped shoulders, Shaun trudged to Ryan, handed him Mick's leash, then took the key from Lacey.

"This probably isn't the best time to check your security. I'll make sure I come over while it's daylight, possibly at lunch tomorrow. Okay?"

"That's fine with me. We're interviewing for a maid position tomorrow, but that's early in the morning." Lacey moved toward the door and faced him. "Thanks for dinner tonight."

For a couple of seconds, she paused, her gaze trained on him, and all he wanted to do was kiss her. In the few days he'd known her, she'd dominated his thoughts, even while on the job. "Good night." He waited until she was inside before leaving.

He'd been seriously involved with a woman while an FBI agent, but his work kept interfering. He'd traveled a lot and dealt with tough cases that drained him emotionally. When she broke it off, he'd known it was for the best, but it had hurt. In the four years since then, he'd only casually dated, keeping every relationship at arm's length.

As he entered the house, his phone in the kitchen rang. He picked it up, for some reason thinking it might be Lacey. He still said, "Sheriff McNeil," because his office always called his landline when he was at home.

"Deputy Ferguson here. A murder victim was found half a mile north of your house in a wooded section on the left side of the road."

Too close to home. "I'll be there."

FOUR

"Who do we have?" Ryan asked as he climbed from his SUV.

"Don't know and it'll be hard to get an ID on him. The body's still where it was found." Deputy Ferguson led the way through the trees. "The grave was shallow enough that the Dickerson's German shepherd's digging exposed the victim."

"When was the body discovered?"

"Seven. Cal Dickerson was returning from walking his dog. When he gets close to his property, he lets Duke off his leash. The German shepherd likes to cut through the woods and beat Cal home. When Duke starts barking and doesn't quit, Cal knows something's wrong. He hurries home and gets a flashlight and then goes looking for his dog. It takes a while to locate him because he's stopped barking. Cal finds the dog guarding the partially revealed body."

Duke was one of the local SAR dogs they used when they needed to search for a missing person. "Where are Cal and Duke?"

"I sent them home after interviewing Cal. He was pretty shaken up. The body hadn't been in the ground long, but the killer didn't want the victim identified. At least that's my opinion." Deputy Ferguson entered the taped off section of the woods.

When Ryan viewed the body, he understood his deputy's comment about the killer. "The murderer must have used some kind of acid on his face and hands." He'd seen a lot of dead bodies, but this one was especially nasty. It took him a minute to shut down his emotions in order to search the area for any clues that would lead them to the perpetrator.

He could count on one hand the murders committed in his county since he became sheriff three years ago. "Any ID on the body?"

"Nothing. Not even clothing tags."

"Do you think this man could have been part of the burglary ring, and he had a falling out with the others?" Deputy Ferguson asked, turning away from the body.

"Maybe. First thing tomorrow morning, I'll be interviewing the two men we arrested again. Now with murder possibly being connected to the burglaries, one of them might talk for a deal. Have all the photographs been taken? If so, the body needs to be transported to the Maryland Medical Examiner's Office."

"They're on their way to pick up the body."

Ryan scanned the woods beyond the lights brought in to illuminate the dumpsite. Menacing darkness loomed yards away.

* * *

Ryan sat next to one of the jailed burglars,

Don White. He'd already interviewed his partner who had little to say. That man had already served time for a burglary charge. White had never been in prison, and so far he hadn't requested a lawyer. Ryan would play on those two things.

"We found one of your cohorts last night—dead. He died painfully, his face eaten by acid. The crew you work for doesn't play nice." Ryan lowered his voice to a conspiratorial level. "Listen, you haven't ever been convicted, let alone charged with a crime. If you give us information to help us bring in the rest of your gang, I'll get the DA to give you a break. Maybe no prison time. Possibly house arrest and probation."

"I can't help you. I don't know anything." White rubbed his hands together over and over.

"Let me be the judge of that."

"I was hired to pick up a guy. That was all. I knew nothing about a burglary. How can that help you?"

"Hired to pick up someone? How? Who hired you?"

"I'm part of PAC."

"A personal automobile chauffeur in the D.C. area?"

White nodded.

"Why didn't you tell me this the other day?"

"Mr. Johnston told me not to say a word or else. He would take care of everything. But since I've been sitting in jail, I've kinda figured he has no intention of taking care of me. I know nothing except what I've told you."

"How many times have you picked up someone here?"

"He's been my only one."

"Where were you taking him?"

White shrugged. "D.C. That's all I know. He was gonna tell me more when we were closer."

The burglary ring was based in D.C.? The homes they had hit belonged to wealthy people who lived outside the capital. Maybe the dead guy they'd found in the woods had nothing to do with the burglaries.

Ryan wrote out a series of dates when

the burglaries took place. "Put down where and who you were with at those times. Is there a person who can give you an alibi?"

White pointed to two dates on the paper. "Yes, that day and that one, too."

"Good. When you're through, knock on the door and give the sheet to the officer. He'll take you back to your cell."

Ryan left and gave the guard instructions. Then he needed to leave the station. Take a break. See Lacey. Especially after the night he'd spent at the dumpsite.

* * *

Lacey talked with the painter about the change to the color scheme in the Greene Suite. Then she made her way to the office to finally have a word with Mrs. Bell. She had an idea that might make the situation a little better. The atmosphere in the kitchen as Shaun hurried to get breakfast and make the school bus had been tension filled to the point her son didn't say a word until she walked with him to the front porch.

She paused at the entrance into the office and dragged air into her lungs. The bed and breakfast had been an answer to her prayers. She'd thought her worries were over with her unexpected inheritance from Mr. Hopewell. She'd been wrong. New concerns replaced the old.

Lacey entered the room.

Mrs. Bell lifted her head briefly then returned her attention to the paper in front of her. "Did you need something?"

Lord, give me the right words to say.

Lacey walked to the chair in front of the desk and sat. *Yes, your undivided attention*. Although those words were on the tip of her tongue, she took several deeper breaths then said, "Now that Shaun and I have been here a few days, and I've become familiar with the bed and breakfast, I believe you were right about us staying in the carriage house. But with some changes. I talked with Tom Avant this morning, and he told me what I want can be done after he finishes the main house."

Mrs. Bell straightened, her back so stiff it appeared she had a broom handle instead of a spine. "What changes?"

"To transform the carriage house into one unit with a kitchen, living room and two bedrooms. It would be our home. I still want to be heavily involved in the bed and breakfast. I thought we could talk about what my part will be here. You and Richard are important to the Calvert Cove B and B. I have a lot to learn from you. Tell me what your favorite parts of your job are?"

Surprise flickered into the woman's eyes, and she sank back against her chair. "Doing the books, ordering, tasks behind the scene."

"Ah, great. I would love dealing with the staff and the guests. I was a receptionist in my previous job and enjoyed interacting with others. We could each do what we like the best." Lacey still had more to talk to Mrs. Bell about, but she didn't want to overload the woman. She rose.

"When are you and your son moving out to the carriage house?"

Lacey knew Mrs. Bell wanted her to move today, but since there were no guests at the bed and breakfast for several weeks, she had decided to wait until her renovations to the carriage house were complete. "As soon as our place is ready for us." At the entrance into the office, she glanced over her shoulder. "I've made a few changes to the colors scheme in a couple of the suites. The painter and contractor already know what I want."

She quickly left before Mrs. Bell said anything to spoil what Lacey felt had been a successful meeting.

Richard wrote something on a pad then looked up at her. "Anything special you want in the way of food? Does Shaun have favorite snacks?"

"Apples and bananas. I never could keep enough for him."

He scribbled on the paper. "How about you?"

She grinned. "Anything you make is a treat for me. I'd love to cook like you." In her small apartment with two hot plates and one toaster, her meals could be limited.

"Then you can assist me at dinner if you want. Nothing I like better than sharing my love of cooking with another."

"You've got yourself an assistant then." Lacey crossed to the back door.

Richard joined her. "I usually purchase groceries twice a week. Tuesday is one of the days. Friday, the other one."

"That's good to know in case I need something special."

After Richard closed the door behind him, he descended the steps beside her. "I overheard a few things you and Harriet talked about. I feel you need to know a little about her. Ten years ago my wife was pregnant with our first and only child. At eight months, he stopped moving. When she went to see the doctor, she found out that our child had died. She still had to go through labor to deliver a dead baby. After that, Harriet changed. She didn't want to try and have another child. Since then, she tolerates the children of the guests. She doesn't want to be around kids. I wanted you to know that Shaun hasn't really done anything wrong. Your decision for you and Shaun to live in the carriage house would be better for Harriet, but I believe for you and your son also."

"Less tension?"

Richard nodded, a shine to his eyes. "I love my wife, but something inside her died the day we lost our son."

Lacey didn't know what to say. Her throat thickened around each word she thought might be appropriate, but if she'd lost Shaun in childbirth, she imagined she would have a huge hole in her heart, too. She swallowed several times before she said, "Thank you for letting me know. Shaun can be active and overzealous at times. Besides, I'm thinking of getting him a dog. Our living in the carriage house would be better for all involved."

"See you at five in the kitchen." He headed for the bed and breakfast's SUV.

Now she had time to go through the carriage house and make sketches of how she wanted to remodel it. Then she would show them to Tom and see if what she envisioned was doable.

As she strolled to the building, she found a perfect place for a fountain and pond to be located. She would talk with the gardener tomorrow to see if Gus could put one in.

She paused and relished the sweet scent of honeysuckle and gardenia bushes near the entrance into the carriage house, soon to be her new home. The sun's warmth bathed her. A light breeze played with the strands of her hair. Not a cloud in the sky. In the past, she'd rarely stopped what she was doing to savor the moment.

But she did now.

Tranquil. Invigorating. A haven after living in the midst of a gang-infested war zone.

She sighed and unlocked the main door with her key. She would have Tom knock out the short hallway walls and open up the place. She stopped in the entrance to the suite on the right. It would be where her living room, dining area, and kitchen would be. When she put its key into the lock and turned it, she found it already open. Strange. Each interior door to the two suites were kept locked as well as the outside one.

Maybe the last time she'd been here,

she'd forgotten to secure it properly. With her distracting thoughts of Ryan, she could see where she might have. She hadn't dated since her husband died, but that had been her choice. She'd had several offers, but she'd totally messed up her first choice and didn't want to do that a second time.

As she entered the suite, anticipation of the possibilities for her life and her future home surged through her with excitement.

Until she saw the walls riddled with holes in them.

What in the world...

What if the person who made these is still here?

FIVE

"Sheriff McNeil here." Ryan recognized the number of the bed and breakfast.

"Ryan, this is Lacey. Someone broke into the carriage house and made a bunch of holes in the walls."

"Where are you now?"

"When I saw the vandalism, I fled to the main house."

Ryan increased the speed of the car. "I'm almost there. Stay where you are."

Holes in the walls? Why?

A few minutes later, Ryan drove into his driveway, parked, and hurried to the bed and breakfast. Keeping his gaze on the carriage house, he knocked on the kitchen door. It opened immediately.

"You weren't kidding about being almost here, and I'm glad. I've been keeping an eye on the door into the carriage house. No one has come out."

"There are other ways. You stay here while I go through the place."

"But, I—"

"Stay here."

She trailed him to the rear door.

He rotated toward her and leaned against the exit. "Don't even go out on the patio. We don't know what's going on. No reason to put yourself at risk."

"How about you?"

He clasped the butt of his gun in his holster at his side. "I've been trained to deal with these types of situations. Do I need any keys?"

"In case you do, here." Lacey thrust the keychain into his hand.

Her touch set off myriad sensations zipping through him. "Did you go into both suites?"

"Only into the one on the right. I didn't

go that far into it."

He turned his back on her. "Good. You didn't disturb the scene—much."

He strode to the carriage house, approaching the first suite cautiously. The door wasn't locked. He took out his gun and moved into the living area. The Swiss cheese walls went throughout the suite, even in the bathroom. The holes were no more than two inches in diameter from his waist down to the floor. All the windows were locked.

After Ryan crossed to the suite on the left, he found the same scene in the large sitting area but the bedroom didn't have many holes in the wall. The window in it, facing away from the main house and toward Chesapeake Bay, was unlocked. When had the burglar done this? Last night? During the daytime?

No, the intruder most likely was interrupted with Lacey's appearance because the walls weren't riddled with holes in this bedroom.

Was this part of the burglary ring that had been plaguing the area for the past month?

Probably not. The MO wasn't like any of the other places hit. This took time. With the other burglaries, the thieves had entered at different times, day or night, only staying there less than half an hour.

Something else was going on here, whether the ring was involved or not.

Ryan returned to the kitchen to find not just Lacey but Richard and Harriet standing at the island counter, waiting for him. "Both suites are similar except for one bedroom. There weren't a lot of holes there."

Lacey paled. "He was in there when I was. I could have..."

Ryan covered her hand on the counter. "But the intruder left rather than confront you. You're all right." He wanted to comfort her more, but he was determined to get to the bottom of the break-in. "I'm calling one of my deputies to help me process the scene. It's obvious whoever's responsible for making the holes was searching for something. Do any of you know what it might be?"

"Bugs," Richard said with a shrug.

Harriet punched him in the upper arm. "This isn't a joking matter."

"So your contractor wouldn't be looking for damaged pipes or something?" Ryan asked, although it was unlikely. He had to rule out what he could.

All three shook their heads.

"Where is Tom?" Ryan withdrew his cell phone.

"Checking the third floor. His workers completed it this morning. I'll go get him." Lacey headed into the hallway.

"I'm trying to remember any work done, not counting cosmetic changes, on the bed and breakfast other than when it was renovated extensively nineteen years ago. I can't, but then I wasn't here some of that time." Ryan speed-dialed his office.

"No, other than the pipes replaced on the first floor bathroom and kitchen ten years ago. And nothing with the carriage house." Harriet moved to the coffeepot and held it up. "Want any?"

"No," Ryan said while the phone rang. When his receptionist/secretary answered, he requested the nearest deputy be dispatched to the bed and breakfast.

Lacey and Tom came into the kitchen. "I'd like to take a look at what was done," he said when Ryan finished his call.

"Me, too," Harriet said.

Ryan held up his hand. "After I process the carriage house, I want you all to go through the crime scene and tell me what you think."

"It couldn't be any of my workers. No reason to. Plus I keep a close eye on what they're doing." Tom poured himself a cup of coffee. "I'll finish up the third floor inspection then come back down." He glanced at Lacey. "I guess it's a good thing you were going to redo the carriage house."

Ryan remembered seeing some workers there working last week. "Redo the carriage house? Weren't those renovations already completed?"

"Shaun and I are going to live there once the two suites are combined into one unit. It'll seem more like our own home." Lacey exchanged a look with Harriet.

Had something happened between them? "After I'm finished with the carriage house, I'll do a walkthrough the whole place with an eye on security. That's why I was headed here when you called."

"Good. The carriage house, too." Fear leaked into her expression.

He wanted to make her feel better. Any intrusion was a violation—very personal. For some it changed how they felt about a place. "Definitely."

As he strode to the carriage house, he couldn't shake the need to protect Lacey and her son. He didn't have a good feeling about what was going on. Why holes in the walls? Looking for something?

* * *

That evening on the patio, surrounded by the beautiful gardens filled with roses, azaleas, and hydrangea bushes, Lacey should feel at peace, content. The location and weather alluded it. The main house was going to reopen on time. And now that the sun had set an hour ago, the discreet lighting illuminated the surroundings just enough to allow a person to enjoy the colorful flowers but with a sense of privacy as though no one else was around.

But Lacey knew better.

After the lurker the other day and now the vandalism in the carriage house, it was evident someone was watching the B and B. The thought shivered down her length. Her gaze landed on the door into the place she was going to make her home.

When Ryan returned from talking on the phone to a deputy at the station, he sank onto the wooden bench next to Lacey. "I hope there're no more calls tonight. Nothing good comes from them."

"What's going on?"

"That was Deputy Ferguson. Johnston, one of the burglars we caught, jumped White, the other one."

"A falling out between thieves. That might not be so bad."

"No, I don't think White is actually part of the ring. I've separated him from the other inmates."

"Do you think what happened today is

part of what's going on in the area?" She shifted so she faced him on the bench. She'd thought coming to the bed and breakfast would make her feel safe, that she'd be able to protect her son.

"That's a possibility, but in my gut, I don't feel it's connected. Most of the robberies have been similar. With you, nothing's been taken. Just vandalism."

"That doesn't make me feel better. And for the record, we don't know that something wasn't found. Maybe the intruder was here during the night, got what he was looking for, and left, not bothering to close the bedroom window. But then what he took would have to be small to fit through a hole."

He cupped her hand between his. "I know. I wish I could assure you that you'll be okay. I can't. I'll do all I can to keep you safe. That's my job, but after years of being in law enforcement, I have to admit that there's no guarantee you will be. I can't control that. It sounds cynical, but it's also freeing. I have to turn your well-being over to the Lord. That doesn't mean I don't do the best job I can. It means I don't waste time worrying about the future."

"For years, that's all I've been doing, worrying about how I was going to pay off my deceased husband's debts and keep a roof over our heads and food on the table. I thought when I received this inheritance that, finally, my life was turning around. I'm not afraid of hard work. I've been doing it since I became an adult. But this unknown threat has come out of the blue. Neither of us has any idea what's going on. How do I *not* worry?"

"Pray. Ask God for help. I promise that all your worrying won't change the outcome. In fact, when I did worry a problem to death, I made it worse. Once, in a case as an FBI agent, I tried to force a solution that, in the end, almost got my partner killed. That's when I left the job and reassessed my life."

That was all she'd been doing—trying to force what she wanted. She'd had no choice but to repay the money her husband owed after his death, or the unsavory person would have come after her and

Shaun. The lack of control over her circumstances nearly drove her over the edge, especially when neighbor kids ganged up on Shaun. Then she'd received the notification from the lawyer about her inheritance from Mr. Hopewell. She hadn't even known who he was until she met with the attorney. She'd thought she'd been given a second chance, but now she wasn't so sure.

Ryan gently squeezed her hand. "Are you okay?"

"You've given me a lot to think about. For so long, my life has been out of control or so I thought because things weren't going the way I wanted. I had a vision of what my life should be, but I wasn't even near that goal. Maybe instead of planning for the future, I should live in the moment and relish the present."

He gave her a lopsided grin. "I've been there. It's not easy savoring the here and now and letting the future take care of itself. I wish I could say I have this not worrying down pat. I don't, but I'll keep working on that."

"I know one thing. I'm glad the sheriff lives next door to me."

His words and smile made her feel not so alone. In order to make this move, she'd given up her friends and neighbors. Although, this area had been her home at one time, she didn't expect to see many people from her past since she'd only been twelve when her family moved. Ryan had been a pleasant surprise.

"I didn't get a chance to ask earlier, but what made you decide on moving into the carriage house? Are you still going to?"

She nodded. "We should live there. Harriet and I have come to a compromise. Part of that is the decision to live in the carriage house."

"Why?"

"Did you know Harriet had been with child and lost the baby?"

He shook his head.

"Richard told me. The boy would have only been a few years older than Shaun. She needs space and time to get used to the fact Shaun is living here. Besides, I want to get a dog for him, and the carriage house would give us more privacy and be a better place to have a pet, especially with guests staying in the big house."

"Most people love animals."

"I'm not going to hide the dog, but there are some who don't like pets or are allergic to them. Depending on the situation, the carriage house gives me options when people like that are staying here."

"I'll call my friend with the cocker spaniel and see if he has any left. If so, we could go see if that's what Shaun wants."

"If my son wasn't asleep, he'd be jumping up and down, celebrating. I'll tell him when you have something set up. I've been reading about cocker spaniels. They sound like a good match for him."

Ryan rose. "I'd better go. If I'm lucky, I won't get a call in the middle of the night about another burglary or worse."

She stood, wishing he wasn't going home. His presence calmed her, especially after the news of the murder, but she needed to find that within herself. "Did you discover who the man in the woods was?"

"Not yet. He was strangled. We're trying to ID him with a forensic artist. In the meantime, we'll keep track of any missing people in a fifty-mile radius. If that doesn't work, we'll expand the scope of the search. The murder could be tied to the burglary ring."

He closed the small space between them. "Your door is only yards away, but I'm escorting you to your suite. And it's not because I think you're in danger right now. I want to. This house's security system isn't bad. A few updates and changes will make it better, but a bed and breakfast isn't the same as a home. You have guests who come and go throughout the day."

"But I can make the carriage house like Fort Knox."

"Remember what I said about worrying." He cradled her face between his large palms.

In the soft lighting, his expression melted her insides. All she wanted to do was wrap her arms around him and keep him right there in front of her. She hoped he would kiss her. His lips were so near.

She remembered thinking about him when she was twelve and her big sister had a crush on him. Everyone liked him, but to her he'd been unattainable. He was fifteen and in high school. Popular.

He bent toward her, his mouth barely touching hers. Goose bumps flashed down her arms. Then his fingers combed through her hair and held her head still while his lips set out to devastate her equilibrium. She tightened her hold on him and pressed closer, needing him to keep her upright.

Their kiss awakened something that she'd thought died in her after a few years of marriage. Passion. Hope. Fulfillment.

When his mouth no longer covered hers, she didn't want it to end. But it had been a long day for Ryan, and he had a lot to deal with—probably tomorrow, too.

"I'll call in the morning, and maybe in the evening we can go see the cocker spaniel. I want him to be sure. If that puppy doesn't connect with him, there will be others. We have an animal shelter not too far away. It would be a good place with lots of choices for Shaun."

She stood on tiptoes and gave him a quick kiss. "As a friend told me recently, I'm not going to worry about it. See you tomorrow."

After she locked the door to her suite, she immediately went to check on Shaun. He was her life. Whatever was going on at the bed and breakfast, *she* would protect her son.

SIX

"I want this one. No, wait, this one!" Thursday afternoon, Shaun hurried from one cage at the animal shelter to the next. "There are so many to choose from." He finally stopped in the middle of the row, perplexed. "What do I do?"

Lacey strolled from one cage to the next with Ryan, inspecting each dog. "I don't want a dog that's too big since he'll stay inside a lot of the time. Also, I think we should get a young one but not necessarily a puppy." Maybe it was a good thing there were no more cocker spaniel puppies at Ryan's friend's house. They would require a lot more work, especially the house training. She had enough new things in her life and didn't want to take on another. "How about a dog between one and five?"

Shaun read the information on the sign to the left of him. "A lot of the ages are an estimate if the dog's a stray."

"The shelter doesn't close for an hour. Take your time. If you're interested in one, a volunteer will take it out to the play yard for you." Ryan squatted in front of a mixed breed, brown with splotches of white, its tail wagging and its front paws poking through the chain-link door. "She reminds me of a smaller version of Mick. Not in looks as much as temperament."

"Really." Shaun came back to Ryan. "Yeah, she does. What breeds do you think she is?"

"It says Corgi and Bull Terrier. It has the long body, squatty legs of a Corgi and the short hair and face of a bull terrier."

Shaun knelt next to Ryan. "She's friendly."

"Do you want to take her out to the fenced yard to see how you two get along?"

Lacey motioned to one of the workers at the other end of the row.

"Yes." Shaun hopped to his feet.

Two minutes later, Lacey knew that the mutt was perfect for Shaun. He immediately began playing with the mixed breed, first throwing a tennis ball for her to fetch then playing tug-of-war with a rag. Shaun's laughter blended with the dog's yelps.

Standing next to Ryan, Lacey leaned against the side of the building. "I thought we would be here after the place closes because he couldn't choose. How did you know he'd love this one? He ran right by her earlier."

"I have a gift. You could say I'm a dog whisperer."

She chuckled. "You are? Why do you say that?"

"Because I could tell she needed Shaun. He saw it, too."

"Don't make me roll my eyes."

"What? You don't believe me?"

"You were desperate. That was the third row Shaun ran down, wanting to take half of the dogs in them."

"He was like a chocoholic in the middle of a chocolate factory. Too many choices. I narrowed it down for him."

Shaun trotted to them with the dog right beside him. "I'm gonna call her Sadie."

"Are you sure about her?" Lacey asked, although the smile on her son's face indicated he was.

"Yes, and I promise I'll walk her and feed her."

"Okay, then we need to let them know." Before Lacey had a chance to push off the wall, her son hurried to the door into the building and disappeared inside. "I haven't seen him this happy in ages."

"He was five when your husband died. Did he take his dad's death hard?"

"His father had little to do with him. He was either gone on the road playing in a band or jamming with his buddies when he was in town. What was hard for Shaun was the bullies in the neighborhood. If I could have moved, I would have. Paying off my husband's debt was paramount. The men he owed weren't patient. That was my number one priority, or I would never be able to start over somewhere else. They made that very clear."

"So Shaun wasn't the only one being bullied."

"I guess you're right. When I did pay off the debt, I was still scared they'd hold me there with some other kind of threat, but at least the top guy was a man of his word. I can't say that about all of them, but no one crossed him." For an instant, a vision of Remy Gautier popped into her mind. Mean, tough, but honest in his dealings, if a person followed what he dictated.

She had. "For over two years, I worked two jobs. I missed some of Shaun's childhood, but a nice lady in our building watched him when he got home from school. All she asked me to do was clean her apartment as payment. Then I received Mr. Hopewell's legacy. He wanted it to go back to a member of the original family."

"It sounds like you had a guardian angel looking out for you."

Shaun stuck his head out the entrance.

"Mom, we have to leave Sadie here overnight. Their policy before adoption is fixing Sadie so she can't have puppies. I like puppies."

"That policy is in place to keep the number of animals down. The shelter can only handle so many." Lacey followed her son to the receptionist to take care of the adoption paperwork.

Shaun stooped and hugged his dog. "We'll be back after school tomorrow to pick you up."

As they walked out of the building, Ryan said, "Let's celebrate. I don't know about you two, but that's hard work, picking just the right pet. There's a great barbeque restaurant in town. Dinner is on me."

Shaun brightened up immediately.

Ryan seemed to know the right thing to say to her son to cheer him up. He ruffled Shaun's hair as he climbed into the backseat. In that moment, Lacey realized that the county sheriff would make a great dad. Had he ever married? Why didn't he have children? Although they'd been neighbors while growing up, she didn't know a lot about the adult Ryan.

* * *

The following Monday evening on the patio at the bed and breakfast, Ryan unhooked Mick's leash from his collar. "You're free. Go show Sadie what she needs to do." When he said go, his dog made a beeline for Shaun and Sadie at the other end by the recently dug hole. "I see you're getting a pond. When will the gardener have it finished?"

Lacey sat in the lounge chair next to Ryan's in an alcove surrounded on three sides by several butterfly bushes with lovely purple flowers. "By Saturday. Shaun and I are heading to Baltimore for the day. We're going to buy the fish for the pond. You're welcome to come if you aren't working."

"I just might. Let me see what develops with the burglary case. When I contacted PAC in D.C., I discovered their services were used for each of the thefts. I'm going to Alexandria to talk to the other drivers. PAC will contact me if they receive a call from anyone in this part of Maryland, but we had another break-in yesterday afternoon. The driver service wasn't involved. I'm sure the person running the gang has figured out that White has talked."

"How many times has the ring hit the area?"

"Yesterday was the fourth time, farther north on the county line. I've talked with that sheriff, and he's aware they could be moving into his territory."

"How about the guy who stole the boat? Did you find him?"

"No. I've had what little evidence I saw of the man sent to other sheriffs in the vicinity and to all my deputies. But no one has sighted anyone who looks like him. The video cam of the dock where the boat had been moored showed a man of similar description on the pier nearby. I'm ninety percent sure it's the lurker I saw."

"But still no one has seen him?"

"No. Frustrating." Ryan pointed at a

yellow butterfly. "We don't seem to be bothering it while it's feeding."

"They ignore me. I come out here several times a day. I love the different ones that flock to the bushes."

"I may need to get several more butterfly bushes. It's sort of like bird watching. Peaceful."

"Gus has a friend who has different bird feeders. I'm going to buy several and put them in various places in the garden. I think the guests will enjoy watching both the butterflies and birds."

"How's it going with Harriet?"

Lacey slid a glance toward Ryan as he observed another butterfly—black and red—flutter around the cluster of purple flowers. "We take two steps forward and one back."

"It could be worse. One step forward and two back. You're going in the right direction."

"Yeah, and it's only been ten days since we arrived."

One of his eyebrows rose. "Just ten days? It seems like you've been around longer than that."

"Is that a compliment?"

"Of course. It's like you never left."

She laughed. "Hardly. A lot has happened in that time."

He frowned as though a memory from the past caught hold of him and wouldn't let go. "Yeah, a lot. We aren't those carefree kids anymore."

Ryan had shared some of his past with her, but every once in a while, she could tell he hadn't totally left it behind. He was still working at living in the moment and letting the past go. She didn't know if she ever could. "Carefree? What's that? That's called growing up, and sometimes it isn't easy. When I was a child, I couldn't wait to be an adult. Then I could do anything I wanted. I didn't have to follow my parents' rules or the school's."

His face lit with a smile. "Exactly. Then reality hit. We got a whole different set of problems and rules."

Giggles floated to her. Shaun lay on the ground while Mick hovered over him, licking his face. Sadie joined the other dog, lavishing her son with attention. "I can't think of a better place to have come. This would never have been possible at our previous home. There wasn't even a park nearby, and the closest one needed so much work done to it we stopped going, especially when I saw a drug deal going down not twenty yards from the playground."

"I'm glad you're here, too."

She looked at Ryan and couldn't take her eyes off him. Her late husband had been ruggedly handsome and very talented musically. When she'd first met him, those two things captured her attention and blinded her to the darker aspects of Jason's nature that she should have considered before marrying him. When Shaun was born, she'd learned how self-centered Jason was. Her son never knew what it was like to have a loving father in his life, even during the five years Jason was in Shaun's life. What appealed the most to her about Ryan was the way he included and treated Shaun—like Jason should have.

Ryan reached out and ran his fingertips

across her forehead. "What's wrong?"

"Nothing."

"Then why the furrowed brow?"

"Just the past intruding."

"It's behind you. Don't let it rob you of the present."

"You don't ever let that happen to you? Like a few minutes ago?"

"I told you I don't have it down pat yet. I still have flashbacks to dicey situations but not as badly as I used to. When you immerse yourself into the mind of a terrorist in order to figure out his next move, it isn't pretty. There were times I needed to think like one, and it went against all I believed in. The hate, the disregard for human life." He took a deep breath. "But being here in this beautiful garden with you and Shaun means a lot to me. I'll be able to replace those flashbacks with this scene. Much better for me." He leaned toward her and grasped her hand.

Rising, he pulled her up against him. "Maybe we can meet out here later after Shaun goes to bed."

His husky soft voice and devouring look

melted her against him. "I think I can arrange that." He caressed her cheek, dipping his head.

His dark eyes drew her in. For a few seconds, she forgot where she was until a bark sliced through the air. She gasped, stepped back, and looked around Ryan at her son helping Sadie play tug-of-war with Mick. Heat flushed her face. Ryan could make her forget where she was.

"Who do you think will win?"

"Mick. He's got eighty pounds of muscles behind him, and this is his favorite thing to do."

Shaun began to lose ground. "I think you're right for now, but if my son eats much more of Richard's cooking, he'll be putting on more pounds, and Sadie hasn't reached her full size. Did I tell you Richard is giving me cooking lessons?"

"No. Maybe I should ask him to give me some."

"You can always join us. I help him every evening."

"Only if I get to stay and eat one of his meals."

"Anytime." Lacey checked her watch. "And speaking of time, my son has school tomorrow." She walked from the alcove. "You need to go to bed, Shaun. It's already fifteen minutes past eight."

"Ah, Mom. Just a little longer."

"No, at this rate you won't calm down until nine. You have to catch the bus at seven-thirty."

Shaun let go of the sash. Mick pranced around with it still in his mouth.

"That's his victory lap," Ryan whispered in her ear.

The feel of his breath on her neck sent tingles down her spine. She was falling for Ryan. In a short time, he'd broken down all her barriers.

With a pout, Shaun trudged toward her. "This weekend I'll be able to play a lot more. No school, Sadie."

Lacey watched as he and his dog headed toward the door that led to their suite.

When Ryan's cell phone rang, the sound startled her. She glanced over her shoulder at him in the alcove with Mick. His expression morphed into a frown. Not good news.

A minute later, he disconnected and joined her. "I have to go. Someone spotted a man hanging around a house. It could be one of the burglars."

"I hope you'll let me know what happens. I don't care how late it is."

His eyes widened. "Are you sure? It could be midnight or later."

"Yes. I have a vivid imagination and probably won't sleep well anyway. I don't want anything to happen to you."

He leaned down and gave her a quick kiss. "It won't."

Then he and Mick walked away. She didn't take her gaze off Ryan until he disappeared from view. There was heaviness in her chest, as though she wouldn't see him again. Now she knew she wouldn't get any sleep until she heard from him.

* * *

Ryan parked down the road and crept to

the place where two of his officers, Deputies Simmons and Ferguson, waited.

"The Reynolds are out of town, but the neighbor on the left thought he saw a light on in their home office even though it hasn't been on any other night the Reynolds have been gone." Deputy Simmons pointed toward the north side of the large antebellum house.

"Where is Deputy Carter?"

"Keeping watch on the rear of the property with Deputy Washburn."

"Has anyone found a getaway vehicle?"

"Nobody saw one in route."

"Since the alarm didn't go off, I'm assuming it's been disabled like the other two." For one of the four thefts, an intruder walked into a house with the alarm code, but so far they hadn't figured out how the thief got the correct numbers. The third burglary was during the daytime, and the maid let in Johnston, who was now sitting in jail. He'd been wearing a disguise. When he was picked up, he still had the clothes on, but the wig, glasses, and mustache had been removed.

Ryan's cell phone vibrated in his shirt pocket. He quickly answered it. "Did you get the information from the Reynolds?"

"Yes, Sheriff. Their code for the alarm system is 1059. There are three ways into the house—front, back, and garage doors. The windows are bolted and wired to the alarm system and shatterproof."

"Thanks." Ryan slipped his cell phone into his pants pocket. "How long since we received the call?"

"Thirty-five minutes," Deputy Ferguson answered.

"We'll give the intruder another ten minutes then go in if he hasn't come out by then. Most of these robberies are pretty fast." Ryan hated the waiting, but it was part of the job.

Deputy Simmons trained his binoculars on the house. "The Reynolds have some expensive pieces of art."

"Yeah, Charles has a coin collection that cost a small fortune." Ryan remembered seeing it one time.

Ten minutes later, Ryan gave the order to move in closer. When he tried the front door, it was unlocked. "Carter, the front is open," he said over the radio to the deputy guarding the rear.

"The back one isn't."

"Stay put in case the burglar runs out that way. Have Washburn come around front."

"Yes, sir."

As Ryan entered the residence, the alarm beeped two times, letting the thief know that an outside door had been opened. He'd hoped to surprise the man. Now he doubted they would. He and Simmons went to the left to clear the rooms while the other two deputies went to the right. Each room Ryan approached, his senses heightened for any indication that something was off. Once, in a similar situation, he'd discovered a suspect hiding in a small cabinet. Somehow he'd squeezed himself into the cramped quarters.

While Simmons remained to cover the lighted hallway, Ryan made his way systemically from one room to the next, clearing them until he reached the office at the end with the door shut. Ryan's heartbeat revved, pumping more adrenaline through him. He plastered himself against the wall then reached around and grasped the knob. He turned it, inhaled a calming breath, and with gun raised, stepped into the entrance. When he flipped the switch up, illumination brightened every corner of the large office.

Ryan assessed the room's hiding places, wanting to clear those first. Cautiously he circled the office, checking behind the curtains, in a small space between a bookcase and the wall, and under a cutout middle section in the big mahogany desk. Sounds of a scuffle in another part of the house momentarily caught his attention. His first instinct was to charge out of the office and see what was going on, but he still needed to inspect the closet and behind the couch. Then he could leave, knowing the left wing on the first floor was cleared.

Every sense focused on any sound or movement in the room, he continued slowly, gun pointed toward the floor. He crept toward the sofa, swinging his gaze between it and the closed closet door six feet away.

Simmons appeared in the entrance. "We caught the thief with some of the artwork in the dining room."

"Okay, call in another deputy to take him to the station. Then have them search the second floor."

"But, Sheriff, in the other thefts, we thought it was done by one thief. It certainly was with Johnston."

"We finish our job here."

His deputy could be right, but Johnston had let slip there were others in the burglary ring. That meant two or more.

While Simmons left, Ryan returned his full attention to the area behind the couch. Suddenly the closet door burst open, and a man with a short, stocky build, like the lurker at the bed and breakfast, charged toward Ryan, plowed into him, and sent him flying back against a bookcase. His head struck against a shelf before he collapsed to the floor.

The blond-haired man stared at him a second then twirled around and raced toward the hallway. Ryan scrambled to his feet, but the room spun around, and he could only stagger forward.

He had to catch this intruder—find out if he was the one at the Calvert Cove B and B. He took two steps forward, sank to his knees, then toppled over.

SEVEN

Midnight and still Lacey hadn't heard from Ryan. She paced the kitchen while her water boiled for tea. Every time she passed the window that afforded her a view of his house, she looked out for a moment, wishing she could see lights on inside or headlights from his SUV nearing his home. Nothing.

Deep down she knew something was wrong. *Please, Lord. Let him be all right*. Her tender new feelings toward Ryan ached with a desperate need to hear from him. Several times she took out her cell phone and punched in his number, but she stopped at completing the call. What if her call distracted him at an important time?

They were neighbors and friends. That was all. She could wait.

Then she would think about the dead man who hadn't been identified yet. He died only a few miles from the bed and breakfast. What if his death was tied to the burglary ring?

The whistle of the water on the stove blasted the air at the same time her cell phone rang. She quickly hurried to the stove and took the pot off the burner while answering the call.

"Ryan, is everything okay?"

"Ma'am, this is Deputy Simmons. The sheriff asked me to call. He was taken to the Calvert Regional Medical Center."

She sank against the counter, her eyes sliding closed. "What's wrong with him?"

"He has a deep gash on the back of his head from an encounter with one of the thieves."

"How bad?"

"The doc is running tests right now."

"I'll be right there." She hung up before the deputy could tell her not to come. If nothing else, she needed to see for herself that he would be all right. Head injuries could be dangerous.

She quickly turned off the burner, hurried to her suite, and changed into jeans and a long sleeve T-shirt. Then she headed across the hall to do one of the hardest things she'd done in a while. She knocked on the Bells' door until Richard answered. She was glad it was him, not Harriet. She couldn't deal with any more drama.

"What's happened?" Richard asked.

"Ryan's been hurt, and I want to go to the hospital. Will you please watch Shaun?"

"What's going on, Richard?" Harriet stepped up behind him.

When her husband quickly told her, Lacey prepared herself for a catty comment that she had no business leaving her son in the middle of the night to see about Ryan.

Instead, Harriet said, "Stay with Shaun. I'll go with Lacey to the hospital. She shouldn't go alone. My goodness, it's way past midnight."

Stunned, Lacey never thought that the woman would offer that. Surprisingly,

Lacey welcomed the company on the ride. She knew where the medical center was, but in the dark, she might get turned around.

In the car, Lacey told Harriet what little she knew about Ryan's condition.

Harriet tsked. "He needs to take it easy. He puts in long hours as our sheriff. Maybe this will make him get some well-deserved rest."

"I hope you can persuade him. I'm glad you came."

"You're good for Ryan," Harriet said after a few minutes of silence.

Lacey was speechless as she pulled into the parking lot next to the emergency entrance. Finally, after switching off the car, she asked, "Why do you say that?"

"Because I've seen him pause and spend time with you and Shaun. I've always thought he should be a father. He's great with kids. Every May, he goes around to the elementary schools in the county to talk to the classes about safety and what they should do in certain situations, especially with summer vacation coming up. Some of my friends have raved about his demonstrations."

Ryan would be a good father—especially for Shaun, who never really had a dad there for him. Was that why she was interested in her neighbor? He'd shared some of his past with her, but did she really know Ryan as an adult? With Jason she'd thought she knew him right from the beginning. She'd been wrong.

"I see Deputy Simmons leaving. Let's catch him before he goes." Harriet climbed from Lacey's car.

Quickly, she followed Harriet, who caught the deputy near his patrol vehicle. "What's the latest on Ryan?"

"A concussion. I'm going to the station to process the two thieves we caught tonight while the doc tries to convince Ryan to go home and rest for a few days. He wanted to keep him overnight, but Ryan said no. He keeps telling them he has a headache. That's all."

"Thanks, Deputy Simmons. We'll take it from here." Harriet charged toward the entrance.

The officer chuckled. "I almost feel sorry for the sheriff. Good thinking bringing her with you. 'Night."

As the deputy slid into his patrol car, Lacey rushed after Harriet and caught sight of her making a beeline for one of the rooms nearby. Ryan must be in there. She went after Harriet as her manager barged inside a room, leaving the door wide open.

"Where's Lacey?" Ryan asked when he saw Harriet.

"I'm right here." Lacey entered, and the doctor left.

Standing on the far side of the bed, Harriet put her hands on her waist. "Deputy Simmons is very capable of handling the thieves. Lacey and I are here to take you to the bed and breakfast."

Ryan's eyebrows rose at Harriet's no-nonsense tone.

Lacey suppressed a smile, and when Ryan swung his gaze to her, she added, "What she said so efficiently."

"You brought back-up?"

"Yes. Richard is staying with Shaun, and it's our job to see you get some rest—as the doctor has ordered."

"Your job? I'm not a chore." He cocked a grin and sat up, swinging his legs off the side of the bed. He started to stand, winced, and sank back down.

"Now do you see why Harriet and I are here? You aren't walking out of the hospital. I'm going to bring my car to the door while someone gets you a wheelchair."

"But one of my deputies brought my car here. I can—"

Lacey put her fingers against his lips. "You might as well accept our help."

"Yes, Ryan," Harriet said. "I can drive your car home."

"Okay, ladies. I know when I'm cornered."

Lacey glanced at Harriet. "I'll go get my car." Which was the easy job. Harriet would have to get Ryan into the wheelchair.

A few minutes later, a nurse and Harriet assisted Ryan into the front seat. He laid his head back against the seat rest, his eyes sliding closed. In the overhead dome light, an ashen cast paled his complexion and a tightening about his mouth when Harriet shut the door made Lacey even more thankful for Harriet insisting he stay at the B and B. He certainly didn't need to be home alone. What if he slipped into a coma or passed out?

"Okay?" Lacey asked as she waited for Harriet to find Ryan's vehicle and pull up behind hers.

"No, but I'll feel better when we get home."

When we get home. For a fleeting moment she had visions of them married, and surprisingly, the thought didn't send her into a panic. Since her husband died, she hadn't even wanted to date, let alone get serious about a man. But could she let herself fall in love with a man who constantly put his life in danger?

* * *

A herd of horses stampeded through Ryan's head. He reached for the glass of water and bottle of painkillers on Lacey's nightstand. He took a pill and swallowed it down with the water. Through the slit in the curtain, a ray of light slanted across the bed coverlet. Daytime. He needed to get to the station and interrogate the burglars, especially the short, stocky one. Ryan was sure he was the one he'd chased to the boat. The idea he'd been casing the bed and breakfast chilled him. He wanted to make sure they had the whole gang. He didn't want anyone else coming to Calvert Cove B and B to steal or hurt someone he cared about.

He flipped back the coverlet and a whiff of Lacey's vanilla scent wafted to him. That smell had haunted his restless sleep last night. As he swung his legs off the bed, the door opened as though Lacey had known he was going to get up. He stood on shaky legs and gripped the bedpost.

She hastened to him as he swayed. "Deputy Simmons is here to see you. He knew you would want a report on what he discovered last night."

"Why don't you have a clock in here? What time is it?"

"Ten in the morning."

"I should have been at my office hours

ago."

"That's why I took the alarm clock out of here."

He eased down onto the bed, closing his eyes as the room tilted.

"I'll have the deputy come back later."

He grasped her arm. "No. I need to know what's going on. Send him in."

She assisted him into a comfortable reclining position. "Everything is being taken care of. Richard went over and brought a few things you might need. Your duffel bag's over there." She pointed to a chair with flower-covered material. "Shaun is taking care of Mick. He thought he could stay home from school in case you needed him, but I told him I'd look after you and Mick until he returned. I'll be right back with the deputy."

He heard her words, but it took a moment to register their meaning. His dog was in good hands. In fact, he was, too, but he didn't have the time to lie around all day and rest. He sat up straight and waited for his pain meds to take effect.

The door opened. Deputy Simmons

entered the room. "Mrs. St. John said not to stay too long. That you need your rest."

"You're not leaving until you fill me totally in on what happened after I went to the hospital."

"I assigned two deputies to process the house. The alarm system had been shut down. There were two thieves last night—Keith Drummond and Pete Newel."

"Which one was the thief in the office? He was short and stocky."

"Keith Drummond."

"He was also the one I chased last week from the bed and breakfast. I'm sure of it. I want to talk to him." The throbbing ache in Ryan's head lessened as his deputy talked.

"He's not going anywhere for the time being."

"Have they told you anything useful? Do you think there are any others involved in the burglary ring?"

"It didn't take long for them to cave. They both thought the other was going to get a deal for cooperating. They were the only two left. The Reynolds' house was their last one in this area. Johnston had been their leader. Things began to fall apart once he was caught. But they carried out the original plans. Five places then leave."

"Did you mention the dead man we found in the woods?"

"Yes, and they knew nothing about him."

"That's to be expected. Admitting to being a burglar is one thing and a murderer another. I need you to look into those men's backgrounds. Search where they're staying, especially look for anything to connect them to the John Doe."

"Both are being taken care of. Sheriff, you've trained me well. Everything will be fine while you recuperate. "

"How much did Lacey pay you to say that last sentence?"

"Not a thing. But she did serve me a delicious breakfast prepared by Richard while she told me how important it was for you to get rest."

Ryan groaned, yet a part of him liked the idea that Lacey wanted to care for him. And that would be great if he didn't have a burglary ring to wrap up and an unsolved murder. He'd been hoping the two were connected, but what if they weren't? "Check with the ME's office about the identity of our John Doe. If we could get a drawing of what they think the man looked like, that would be more than we have right now. We need to broaden our search area for missing men. Go out another fifty-mile radius."

"That'll include all of Washington D.C. and Baltimore. That's a lot of men."

"We have some things that will help us ID him. He had an eagle tattoo on his upper left arm. Circulate that picture around, especially to tattoo parlors. He was also missing one of his top front teeth. We'll use that to narrow our search. The burglary ring was bothersome, but a murder is much more serious."

Deputy Simmons checked his watch. "Oops. My time is up."

"What do you—?"

A light rap then the door opening cut off Ryan's question. Lacey came into the room carrying a brown bag. "I hope everyone at the station enjoys these sweet rolls."

Simmons grinned from ear to ear. "Anything Richard cooks will be greatly appreciated." He took the sack from Lacey. "Sheriff, I'll keep you updated on what we discussed. I'll see you later in the week."

The deputy scurried out of the room so fast Ryan had no time to form a retort. "Lacey St. John, have you resorted to bribing my deputies?"

She smiled. "Whatever it takes. If you'll rest today, you won't hear a peep out of me unless you take a turn for the worse."

He relaxed back against the stacked pillows, chuckling. Since he'd gone away to college, he hadn't had a woman fuss over him like his mom used to. He had to acknowledge Lacey was right. If he rested today, he would heal much faster, and he had too much to do to be laid up for long. "You've got yourself a deal, Nurse Lacey."

* * *

The next morning when Lacey returned to the kitchen after watching Shaun catch the school bus, the aromas of coffee and baking bread vied with the scent of bacon cooking on the stove. She paused, taking in Richard, who whipped up an omelet while Harriet sliced strawberries. He served breakfast to the workers before they began their jobs.

"You two are a good team. Can I help?" Lacey crossed to the counter where Harriet stood.

"Other than setting the food out in the dining room, we're ready. The workers will be arriving any moment. In fact, Tom is already here and out in the carriage house."

"He is? I didn't know. Getting Shaun ready for school can sometimes take my total focus, especially when I'm trying to keep him quiet with Ryan still sleeping."

"I can't believe you managed to get him to rest in the first place." Harriet handed Lacey the pitcher of orange juice while she took the bowl of strawberries and headed into the dining room. "Deputy Simmons only came by here three times yesterday."

"It might have been different if they

hadn't caught the rest of the burglary ring." Lacey set the juice on the buffet at the far end.

"True. Richard once had a concussion, and I almost had to tie him up to keep him in bed."

"How long have you two been married?"

"Fifteen years, most of it spent here."

Why hadn't Mr. Hopewell given the Bells the bed and breakfast? She understood he wanted a member of the original family to own it again, but the couple had put so much into the place. "I want to thank you for coming with me to the hospital. Ryan had a hard time fighting us both about coming here so someone could watch over him."

Harriet gave her a rare smile. "We make a good team."

"Yes, you are so right." Lacey started back to the kitchen to get the rest of the breakfast for the workers.

By the time she finished setting the table, Trey Dawson, the painter, entered the dining room, followed by the electrician, Carl Adams, and a new guy who was helping with the carriage house.

Lacey walked up to the stranger, who had a slender build and sandy brown hair cut short. "I'm Lacey St. John, the owner. I'm glad you could help us on such short notice."

He shook her offered hand. "I'm Jeff Glover. I love working on older houses."

"This is definitely that."

While a couple of more workers arrived, Lacey returned to the kitchen. "I guess I can't put it off any longer. I need to make sure Ryan gets up."

As she made her way to the Garden Suite, thoughts of the past two restless nights flitted through her mind. The couch in the sitting area had been comfortable to sleep on, but she couldn't stop worrying about Ryan. He couldn't see the gash in the back of his head, but she could. He might have died that night or slipped into a coma. She'd once known someone who had been in a car accident and was never the same after a traumatic brain injury.

Whenever she had been with Ryan, she'd watched for any signs that his brain wasn't healing right. By the previous evening, Shaun and the dogs had visited him, and he'd been much better. The pain was manageable, and he'd said he wasn't dizzy. When she opened the door to the suite, Ryan exited her bedroom, fully dressed in his uniform.

"Good. You're up. How's your head?"

"It's still there."

"Your head or your headache?"

He laughed. "Both. I'm much better though."

"Do you feel like eating breakfast?"

"That's what woke me up. I could smell it. What did Richard fix?"

"Omelets or scrambled eggs, biscuits, strawberries, and bacon. According to him, nothing fancy."

"It sounds delicious. I'm starving."

"That's because you didn't eat a lot yesterday."

"Well, my appetite has reared its ugly head. Have you eaten yet?"

"I ate with Shaun."

"Is he at school?"

Lacey nodded and stepped into the

hallway between the two basement suites. "He insisted he should stay home and look after you. That's when I told him you'd be going to work."

"What if I say I'm taking another day off?"

"I'd drive you to the hospital. No doubt you're delirious, if you say that." The smoldering intensity of his gaze burrowed into her. "I'm going to drive you to the station. Consider me your chauffeur. The doctor called last night. Later today, he wants to check you again to make sure you're all right. He suggested that you shouldn't drive until he sees you."

"I'm fine. Really."

Lacey went into the kitchen first. "Humor me. He wanted you to stay home today. Knowing you, I told him that probably wasn't going to happen. My driving you is a compromise."

He paused and faced her, moving close. "You do know me well. That's a scary thought."

She tilted her head. "Why? We're friends."

"Are we? I was hoping for a bit more."

His husky words warmed Lacey. She wanted that, too.

Richard walked into the kitchen. "You better get into the dining room before the workers eat all the breakfast."

"I'm going to see Tom Avant at the carriage house. Then I'll be back to drive you to the station." She hurried from the room before he argued about chauffeuring him around.

"We still haven't settled that matter," Ryan said as she closed the door.

Out on the brick patio, she inhaled a deep breath. She wanted a lot more from Ryan than just friendship, too. She couldn't deny that any longer.

EIGHT

In the interview room at the station, Ryan sat next to Keith Drummond, one of the burglars caught two nights before. "Let me repeat myself. Why were you at the Calvert Cove B and B the week before last?"

Drummond shrugged. "Just seeing the countryside. I was thinking of staying there."

"The boat you used was stolen. Know anything about that?"

The suspect's jawline tightened for a few seconds before he relaxed again. "I found it. I thought I would give it a spin."

"So you had nothing to do with setting

it on fire."

"There was a fire?" Drummond stared at the mirror on the wall. "Who's behind the glass?"

"One of my deputies."

"Well, tell that deputy I want to talk to my lawyer. I ain't answering any more questions. My cooperation has ended."

"That's okay. We have photos of you stealing the boat, and since it was set on fire while you stole it, you'll be charged for its destruction. I hope the joyride was worth it." Ryan nodded toward the mirror.

A moment later, Deputy Washburn came into the interview room to take Drummond back to his cell.

After they left, Lacey entered. "So that's how you question suspects. Did you learn anything new?" She sat where Drummond had and shifted toward Ryan.

"From what I saw in the photo we have of him at the dock, I was ninety percent sure it was Drummond. I needed to see his reaction for myself when I asked him about the bed and breakfast. He was the lurker I chased. Since he's in jail, I don't have to worry about you now."

"That's good. Let's see what the doctor says concerning you. Then maybe I won't have to worry about *you*."

Ryan rose. "I can't believe how fast the morning went by."

Lacey walked beside him down the hall and out the rear of the sheriff station. "Did you get everything you needed done?"

"Most, but other than a crisis, I'm calling it a day."

At her car parked in his assigned spot, she stopped and felt his forehead. "Do you have a fever?"

He shrugged. "I can relax, especially now that the burglary case is wrapping up and I know who the lurker at your place was. The threat of him coming back is gone. We're doing all we can about identifying the John Doe. Someone went to a lot of trouble to hide his identity. I suspect when we know who he is we'll figure out the ID of the killer." Ryan slid into her vehicle and slowly began to release the tension gripping his shoulders and neck. He needed a vacation. Other than the occasional long weekend, he hadn't taken any extended time away in the three years he'd been sheriff. "Did they start on the carriage house today?"

Lacey backed out of the parking space. "Yes. Tom doesn't think it will take too long. He hired an extra worker so it can be completed right before we reopen the bed and breakfast. This will be my first home. I don't count the apartments where I lived in New Orleans."

"That's the way I felt when I returned to my house. So many times I was traveling for my job and lived in hotels. I didn't realize how important it was that I put down roots until I did. The retiring sheriff asked me to consider running for his position, or I'm not sure I would have thought to do that."

"This county is lucky to have you."

He'd never looked at it like that. He'd felt he was lucky to have the job. It allowed him to help people and to have a deep connection to a community. Was it time to think about taking that a step further? He'd dated, but until Lacey, it had always been casually. She gave him a reason to pause and consider something more.

She drove into the parking lot at the medical center and found a spot close to the entrance. "After this, let's grab a late lunch."

"Sounds good."

Ryan waited only ten minutes for the doctor to see him. After being told he could work but to be cautious, they left, and he gave Lacey directions to a seafood restaurant.

"This is a fancy place. I'm not sure I'm dressed appropriately." Lacey wore a pair of jeans and a long sleeve blue shirt.

"You look fine to me. It may look fancy on the outside, but it's pretty informal. Besides Richard and your place, this has the best food around. We have something to celebrate. Only the best for our first official date."

She paused, her car door half open. "Date?" A rosy pink brushed across her cheeks.

"Yes. We've been dancing around it for a while. I don't know about you, but I want to get to know you beyond being neighbors. When I was resting yesterday, I had a lot of time to think about you and how in a short time you've become important to me. If you don't feel that way about me, then let me know. That won't affect our friendship."

She held his hand closest to her and laced her fingers through his. "I want more. I never thought I'd say that again after Jason. With the kind of relationship we had, I quickly discovered I would rather be single, but I had Shaun to think about. I wanted him to have a father. Even when my dad lost most of his money, we were still a close-knit family. But Jason didn't understand what it meant to be a dad. I made a promise to myself that wouldn't happen again."

Ryan covered their clasped hands with his free one. "Shaun is a special kid. Whether we're only friends or more, I hope I can be in his life. Besides, Mick wouldn't be happy if he couldn't see Shaun."

"The feeling is mutual."

He exited the car and rounded the hood

as she climbed out. The past few days had been tense, but she gave him hope for the future. He hadn't felt that way in years.

* * *

Lacey stepped into the entrance of Harriet's office. "It is official. We are totally booked solid for May and June and ninety percent for July and eighty-five for August."

The manager glanced up from her computer screen with a huge smile on her face. "And that's because you sent an e-mail out to all our previous customers with pictures of our remodeled bed and breakfast. My favorite is the pond with the goldfish. I think with a big barbeque on the Fourth of July, we might be able to fill that last ten percent quickly. I'll talk with Richard about a menu. Then we can advertise that, too."

"I like that suggestion. Also I wanted you to know that the carriage house is over half done. It should be complete, barring any complications, a day before we reopen. I'll be able to start moving in there a couple of days early while they finish the last room." Lacey couldn't keep the excitement from her voice. She'd felt on top of the world the past week since her first date with Ryan and the soon-to-be completion of the first place she and Shaun could really call a home. When she originally heard the news about Mr. Hopewell's gift bequeathed to her, she'd thought it was a joke, but now it was sinking in that what she'd dreamed of might come true.

"Is Ryan coming to dinner tonight?"

"Yes, he should be able to make it. I told Richard."

"That's nice. I know Shaun loves to have him over here. Your son has settled in quite well since the first few days."

"And I thank you for your patience. He can be a bit … enthusiastic at times."

One of Harriet's eyebrows lifted.

"Okay, all the time when he's nervous. He's making friends, and Sadie has been great for him."

Harriet chuckled.

A door at the front of the house slammed shut.

"Speaking of Shaun. That's him home from school. I promised him we would go look at what's going on in the carriage house."

"But first no doubt, a snack. Richard put something in the fridge for him."

She was halfway across the kitchen when Shaun burst through the doorway. He dropped his backpack on the floor as he came to a skidding halt a foot from her.

"I'm starving. I haven't had anything to eat for *hours*."

"And you might blow away," she opened the refrigerator and pulled out the plate with a ham and cheese sandwich, "unless you get this."

"Thanks, Mom. You're the greatest."

"Richard made it for you, so let him know how much you appreciate the thought."

"Where is he?"

"He's at the grocery store."

Shaun plopped into a chair at the table and dug into the snack. "When can I see the carriage house?" he asked with a mouth full of food.

"Not until you slow down and chew your sandwich."

He really tried to do that, but three or four bites from the end, he stuffed the rest into his mouth then struggled to eat it.

When he finally finished and gulped down half a glass of milk, Lacey settled her fists on her hips and shook her head. "I guess I need to cut your food up until you learn what bite-sized means."

"Ah, Mom. I just wanna see how our place is coming along, especially my room. That way I can figure out what I'm gonna put up on the walls."

"Nothing without my permission. Take your plate to the sink, rinse it, and put it in the dishwasher. Then we'll go."

A moment later, Shaun ran ahead of Lacey and disappeared inside their new home. When she went into the carriage house and didn't see her son, she headed to the left, pretty sure he was in the bedroom designated as his.

"Mom, this is so big," he said over the sound of a hammer striking something in the other part of their new place. "I can have all my friends over for a sleepover. I even have my own bathroom." He dashed into it. "A shower. Great. Baths are for babies." He returned to the main room, caught sight of his closet, the door ajar. "That's huge!" He vanished into it. "Mom, what's this?"

She joined Shaun, who pointed at the ceiling. "Oh, that. I'm glad Tom left it in. That leads to the attic for the carriage house. Aunt Laura and I used to play up there. Originally, the place was used to store hay for the horses."

"Horses. I wish we had a horse."

"Years ago, horses were used to pull the carriages and wagons our ancestors used. Before we leave, I'll show you how your aunt and I would get down."

"Can I go up into the attic?"

"Not now. Maybe one day when I can go with you. I'm not sure what's up there. When we lived here, my parents stored boxes and old pieces of furniture."

"How did you get up there?"

"We used to keep a stepstool in here. We'd use the stool to pull the ladder down."

She gestured toward a metal ring on the ceiling door.

"We might find some kind of treasure up there."

She wouldn't hear the end of it if she didn't show Shaun there was nothing but dust up in the attic. "I'll be right back."

She went out into the living area and found the wooden box she'd seen when she'd come inside the house. Then she borrowed a hammer from one of the workers in her bedroom. After she returned to her son, she stepped up on the box, stretched up toward the ring with the claw of the tool, and hooked it around the ring then pulled down. The ladder unfolded.

Shaun grinned. "It still works. Let's go up and see if there's a treasure in the attic."

"Treasure. I can promise you when we lived here there wasn't any up there."

"You never know, Mom. Maybe Mr. Hopewell left one in the attic."

If she didn't want to be hounded by her son, she might as well give in now. "Okay."

Shaun scrambled up the ladder before

she'd finished agreeing. "What an adventure!"

She hurried right behind him. If there was trouble to be found, Shaun was an expert at discovering it. When her son popped his head through the opening in the ceiling, his body language gave her an answer to what was in the attic, and it wasn't a treasure.

He looked down at her, his shoulders sagging, his mouth set in a pout. "Nothing. Not even one box." Instead of starting to back down, Shaun hauled himself into the attic and his face reappeared in the opening. "But it's a cool place to play. I could make a fort up here. Or I could—"

"Stop right there. In summer, it will be very hot and in the winter very cold." She hoisted herself up through the hole and sat at the edge of the opening with her feet dangling into the closet. All her childhood memories with her sister playing up here flooded her mind. Good recollections. And the weather had never discouraged them. "On second thought, no hotter or colder than outside, especially if we can get a breeze in here."

"And me and my friends wouldn't be bothering any guests." He pointed toward doors at one end that faced the back of the property. "We could open those."

"Yeah, that could help air to circulate."

Shaun rushed toward the east end.

"Wait for me. Don't do anything."

He halted a couple of feet away from his destination.

"In the past, booms had been used to swing the hay to the hole where it was moved inside. When we lived here there was still a rope attached to the boom. We had a tire swing on the end of it." Lacey lifted the plank of wood across the double doors that prevented them from being opened. She swung one toward her and latched it to the wall. "As you can see, the boom and tire swing are gone." But not far from them was a large white oak with branches close by. She could see her son gauging the short gap between the building and the nearest sturdy limb and knew what was going through his mind. "And don't get any ideas about climbing down using the tree. Aunt Laura and I used to climb up it and use the rope to slide down to the tire when the boom was extended. The tree branches weren't this close to the carriage house back then. You can't use it to get in and out of the attic. There will be rules you'll have to follow, or the attic will be off limits."

"Why can't I? The limbs are close now."

"Because going up to a rope only halfway up is different from jumping to a branch and coming all the way down. Understand?"

Shaun nodded then turned away from the double doors to walk the length of the room.

The only light into the attic was one bulb in the middle and a high, small window at the west end, which gave Lacey an idea. Maybe the doors could be replaced with a large window. Then any temptation Shaun and his friends had to jump to the oak would be taken away. Once everything at the B and B settled down, she would talk to Harriet to see if there was any money left to do that additional renovation.

As they returned to the bottom floor, Lacey began to regret telling Shaun about her childhood adventures in the carriage house. If only he hadn't seen the trap door. Until he'd asked about it, she'd forgotten all about it. Thank goodness there wasn't a "treasure" up there. That would have fed his vivid imagination.

Tom showed up when Lacey and Shaun returned to the living area in the carriage house. The contractor explained what was left to do, and they picked out the paint colors for each room. The painter would start tomorrow. Then all that was left of the renovations would be the laying of the carpet and tile. This time next week, she and Shaun would be in their first very own home. Excitement bubbled through her and from the grin on her son's face, him, too.

Lacey left the carriage house a few minutes after Shaun, who went to their Garden Suite to get Sadie. She found Shaun and Sadie with Ryan and Mick talking.

Shaun said an enthusiastic yes as she approached them. "What have you agreed to?"

"We're gonna go for a walk with our dogs."

"Come with us. The temperature is a balmy sixty-eight degrees."

She couldn't turn down Ryan's enticing invitation. "It'll be good to get out. I've been sitting behind my desk most of the day."

As they strolled south on the street, Shaun took both leashes and walked several yards ahead of them.

"How's the murder investigation coming along?" Lacey asked.

"The DNA profile of our victim should be back next week. Then if he's in the database, we'll have a match. That's a long shot, but it might help prove he was a member of the burglary ring. The ones we have in custody all have a record."

"Then what are you going to do?"

"Keep combing the missing persons' lists for a possible match to what the forensic artist thinks the guy might look like. We may never be able to solve the crime." Ryan frowned. "That doesn't sit well with me."

"So you're still thinking the murder is connected to the guys you have in jail."

"I would expect them to deny knowing anything about John Doe. Murder charges are a lot more serious than the ones they face right now. My job would be easier if one of them had killed the guy, but..."

"But what?"

"I don't think they did it, but I need to rule it out." Ryan clasped her hand.

The tactile connection reinforced her growing feelings for him. He was great with Shaun and nothing like Jason. But was that the main reason she was drawn to him in the first place?

"Are you going to have dinner with us tonight?" she finally asked as Shaun detoured into a pasture to let the dogs sniff around.

"Yes, but this weekend, I'm inviting you, Shaun, Harriet, and Richard to dinner at my house. That is, if you'll help me prepare it."

"I'd love to try out some of the cooking skills I've been learning from Richard."

"Good. We'll go shopping together on Saturday."

"Shopping for what?" Shaun asked as he rejoined them.

"Dinner Saturday night at Ryan's place."

"Oh, I almost forgot to ask you if I could spend the night at Ben's that day."

"Sure, but you'll miss our dinner."

Shaun cocked his head. "Ben's having two other friends over for a sleepover. I don't wanna miss the fun." He started back toward the house with the two dogs.

"I've been ditched for Ben," she said with a laugh. "I love it. This will be Shaun's first sleepover. Next he'll tell me he has a girlfriend. I don't want him to grow up too fast."

"I think you have a few years until that happens."

"I remember how you had all the girls following you around when you were in middle school and ninth grade." Her family had left after that, but she doubted that changed.

Ryan chuckled. "He's eight. Don't panic

yet."

"Panic. Should I?"

Ryan stopped and turned toward her, grasping her upper arms and bringing her closer. "No. Shaun may be a bit impulsive, but he's a good kid. Besides, I'll be here to help."

His implication he would be around in the future made her heart soar.

Ryan glanced around then sneaked a quick kiss before continuing their walk while Lacey felt as though she'd stepped onto a cloud and was floating all the way back to the bed and breakfast.

NINE

As Lacey set down her last items from the Garden Suite, the scent of freshly painted walls of silver gray and trim of navy blue suffused the carriage house. It had taken all morning with part of the staff's help to move everything she'd need into the place. She slowly rotated, taking in the gray herringbone chenille couch with navy blue throw pillows and two arm chairs and ottomans. She'd never been able to pick out colors for where she'd lived. Taking in what she had created made her wonder if this was what an artist felt like when they'd completed a picture.

Harriet stood in the entrance to the living room that flowed into the dining area and kitchen, converted from one of the two suites in the carriage house. "Do you need any more help?"

"No. I have all the important boxes unloaded. The others will be emptied when time permits. I'll be at the staff meeting in the dining room in a few minutes."

"See you then."

Lacey made one brief walk through to make sure all the furniture was in the right place. Shaun and she could move some of the smaller pieces but not all of the bigger ones. The second suite had been converted into two bedrooms and bathrooms. She checked out her son's room first, and everything was where it should be, but in hers, the oak bed was on the wrong wall. Maybe this evening Ryan could assist her. The piece weighed nine hundred pounds, and it wouldn't slide on a carpeted floor.

She left the carriage house and crossed the patio to the kitchen entrance. Hot and sweaty from moving, she probably wasn't the most professional-looking owner, but when the time of the staff meeting had been decided a few days ago, they hadn't figured on Trey Dawson being late for work yesterday. He'd had to come back this morning to finish the trim in the carriage house kitchen. But life was full of unexpected events and changes. She was trying not to worry about the past or future. Just live in the moment. It certainly kept her stress level down when she could manage to do it.

Lacey fortified herself with a calming breath then entered the dining room where her two maids, four kitchen and restaurant employees, and a handyman sat, listening to Harriet discuss the changes. When she finished, she turned to Lacey. "As most of you know this is Lacey St. John, the new owner."

Five of the staff had already met her over the course of the past few weeks, but the handyman and one of the maids had been on vacation while the bed and breakfast had been closed for renovations. They were married to each other and had worked here for years.

"We're opening tomorrow to a full house. In fact, for the next four months, we have full occupancy. This is due to the staff and the B and B's stellar reputation. If there's a problem, let me know. Remember you're the backbone at this bed and breakfast. My office door is always open to you all. I'll be handling the staff and guests. Mrs. Bell will be doing all the paperwork and ordering. Welcome to the new employees and welcome back to the others."

After the meeting, the different staff members returned to their tasks in preparation for tomorrow. Every inch of the place would be cleaned for the grand reopening. Lacey walked to her office to finalize a few special requests from guests. She wanted people leaving the bed and breakfast satisfied and recommending Calvert Cove to others.

* * *

Deputy Simmons stepped into Ryan's office. "We finally have a match on our John Doe."

"Who is he?" Ryan put down his pen.

"Trey Dawson. He's a painter who lives in the D.C. area."

"Maybe he was down here for a job. The only out-of-towner in this area was at Calvert Cove B and B, but the work has been completed." Who was their painter? Maybe the guy knew where this Trey Dawson was going to work, or Ryan could call Tom Avant. Tom had been a contractor for over fifteen years, and his reputation was sterling. "I'll contact some people and see if anyone recognizes the photo we received of Dawson. Was it a DNA match?"

"No. A photo and tattoo ID. I'm checking to see if the dental work matches."

"Also, get all the information you can on this guy. Then we'll need to interview the people closest to him. See if someone had a grudge against him." Ryan rose and snatched up his SUV keys. "I'll be at Calvert Cove. If I can catch the painter, he may know something about this Dawson guy."

As he drove toward the bed and breakfast, his spirits lifted with each mile he drew closer. He might have answers to Trey Dawson's murder soon, but best of all, he would see Lacey. The more he was around her the more he wanted to be. He'd spent years traveling for his job, avoiding any commitments because of the nature of his work. Now he'd found someone he could see settling down with. Being with her son made him want to be a father even more.

* * *

Lacey glanced at her watch. Shaun would be home soon. She'd decided to meet him at his bus stop and accompany him to see the carriage house fully furnished for the first time. Plans for his "playroom" in the attic were progressing. Tom had to finish another job then he could make a few changes she could afford right now—mostly replacing the double doors with windows at the east end.

Shaun exited the bus with a group of friends, said something to them, then headed for her. "Is it done? Can we sleep in our new home tonight?"

"Yes. We're going to stay tonight in the carriage house."

"I can't wait until my buddies see it, especially the attic."

"You'll need to wait until the changes have been made to the attic before you and your friends go up there. It's just you and me today, buddy." She put her arm around his shoulder. "I told Harriet and Richard I'm going to cook our dinner at our new home to celebrate."

"Ryan isn't going to have dinner with us? He should be part of our celebration."

The fact that her son had latched onto the dinner part, not the attic part, surprised her. But then why should it? In just weeks, Ryan had become important to Shaun. "If you want to invite him, I'll let you call when we get to the house. I have enough for the three of us to eat dinner." Or she would after she made her spaghetti and meatballs—one of Shaun's favorite dishes. Richard had given her tips to make it even better.

"Can I call him now? I've got to tell him

what I did in gym today."

"Sure." She paused on the patio and withdrew her cell then speed-dialed Ryan's number.

"Hi, Lacey. I was going to call you about your painter. I needed to talk to him. John Doe has been identified. He was a painter in Washington D. C. area. I thought yours might know of him."

"Trey finished a few hours ago, packed up his tools, and left."

"Trey?"

"What's his last name?" Urgency rang through his words.

"Trey Dawson."

"Exactly how long ago did he leave, and do you know where he was going?"

"Before lunch. I'd say eleven-thirty, but I don't know where he was going. He was friendly, but I don't know a lot about him. What's wrong?"

"That's the name of the dead man found in the woods three weeks ago."

Chills streaked down Lacey's body.

"Mom, let me ask him." Shaun held out his hand.

"Just a sec, Ryan." She cupped the phone. She didn't want her son to hear her conversation with Ryan. "Honey, I'll ask him. You go on and see how your room looks."

He hurried the short distance to the door of the carriage house. Lacey waited until he was inside. "Ryan, he's been here all that time. Are you sure the dead man is Trey Dawson?"

"Yes, I just received the final piece of info confirming his identity. He visited a dentist a year ago, and our John Doe's teeth match Trey Dawson's dental records."

"So you think the painter who's been around here killed the real Trey Dawson and took his identity. Why? He was a great worker. He did what he was supposed to, and when he finished, the job looked good."

"I don't know why he impersonated the man, but I need to track down Tom and get an address where the fake Trey Dawson was staying."

She thought of the man she'd been working with to get all the colors exactly right. He was professional and nice—not a murderer. "Could there be two of them?"

"That are painters? Not likely. Either way, I need to talk with the one at the bed and breakfast."

"Will you be able to come for dinner?"

"Sure, unless I have to track down a lead Tom gives me that takes longer than I expect. I'll call you if that happens."

"We'll talk more, after Shaun goes to bed. I'm glad you could ID the John Doe. At least his family will have closure about his disappearance."

After disconnecting, Lacey strolled toward the carriage house while stuffing her cell phone into her pants pocket. When she entered her new home, she paused, again assailed with the smell of paint, which only reminded her of the painter who had done the work. A shiver snaked down her spine. She'd worked with him in the same room only this morning. She was so relieved he was gone now.

She'd thought Shaun would be waiting to make sure Ryan was coming to dinner or at the very least Sadie would have greeted her now. The first thing her son would have done before even going to see his room would be to open the door on the dog's crate. From the time he was home from school until bedtime, Sadie was with him.

She moved into the living area and saw Sadie still in her cage. The dog barked several times and pawed the door. She reached down to open it when Sadie growled and barked again.

"Don't touch that crate." The sound of a voice she'd become familiar with the past few weeks slithered down her spine.

* * *

Glad to see Tom Avant's truck parked in front of the small building, Ryan approached the contractor's office. He'd tried a couple of times to call Tom, but he hadn't answered his cell phone. When Ryan tried the door, it was locked. Maybe the man wasn't here.

Ryan circled the structure to see if there was another way inside that was unlocked. He looked into a window on the south side.

Empty but that was Tom's meeting room. The back door was locked, too. Not having a good feeling about this, Ryan continued his search. On the north side, he peered into another window and spied a pair of legs lying on the floor in front of Tom's desk.

As Ryan rushed to the front, he placed a call to the station, requesting backup and paramedics. Then he went to his glove compartment and retrieved his tools for picking the lock, only used in a case of an emergency—this was one.

Whoever was on the floor could be alive and in need of medical help—or dead.

When he entered the three-room building, he drew his gun. He kept his attention on the closed door to the meeting room as he made his way to Tom's office. The nearer he got, the faster his heart beat. He hadn't seen anyone else inside, but that didn't rule out another person being in there.

He opened the door, slipped into the room, and hurried to Tom on the floor. He felt for a pulse.

TEN

Lacey rotated slowly toward the Trey Dawson imposter, trying to remain as calm as possible, but when she saw the man gripping her son's shoulder as he stood in front of the pretender, her first impulse was to rush to Shaun and grab him close against her. The sight of the gun in the imposter's free hand stopped her—as if she'd frozen in place. Sheer terror gripped her as tight as the man did her son. Shaun's wide eyes and stiff posture showed he was every bit as terrified as she.

She tried to relax her tight muscles. She didn't want to fuel her son's fear any more than it already was. Somewhere deep inside her, she focused on the Lord. He was here with her. She wasn't alone.

A surreal composure replaced her alarm. She had to remain calm if she and Shaun were going to make it through unscathed. "What do you want?"

"I need to search this house without interference."

"What you see is what's in here. You've been here for several days. You should know that."

"It's here. My cellmate told me right before he died."

"You were in prison?" *Stay calm*.

"Yes. I won't harm you two if you do as I say. You're gonna help me find what I'm looking for."

"What is it?"

"A bag. That's all you need to know."

"Where is it?"

"If I knew that, I would have gotten it the first time I looked in here."

What was going to happen if Ryan arrived and discovered they were being held hostage? The imposter had always been nice and respectful. Would he hurt them if Ryan approached? "You made all those holes in the walls?"

"Yes, I used a camera to see behind the plasterboard. I didn't want to sling a sledgehammer just anywhere. It would have heightened the risk of being discovered."

"If you didn't find anything, then maybe the bag is gone. How long has it supposedly been there?"

"Nineteen years ago. It was hidden here when Mr. Hopewell renovated this place the first time. My cellmate was an electrician on the site. He rewired this building."

How was she going to help him? She hadn't lived here at that time. "What's in the bag? How big is it?"

"It's not any bigger than that." The man gestured toward a small teakettle on the counter.

There couldn't be much money in a bag that size. So what? Diamonds or some other gems? Bearer bonds? What it was didn't mean much to her. All she wanted was for Imposter to leave her and Shaun unharmed. "What do you want me to do?"

"Help me find it before anyone comes."

* * *

Tom was alive. Ryan released his breath in relief. After examining the contractor and noticing a wound on his head, Ryan stood and made a sweep of the office first, then the reception area and the meeting room to make sure no one else was in the small building. As he finished up, Deputies Washburn and Carter entered with their guns drawn.

"It's all clear." Ryan holstered his weapon, and the officers did likewise.

"Who's hurt?" Washburn asked.

"Tom Avant was hit over the head. He's unconscious but breathing. After the EMTs take him to the hospital, I want this place processed. I'm following the ambulance. If Tom wakes up, he might be able to tell me what happened."

As Ryan drove toward the Calvert Regional Medical Center, he placed a call to Lacey. Her phone rang and rang until it went to voicemail. "I might be a little late for dinner tonight. I found Tom Avant unconscious at his office. I'm going to the hospital to see if he'll recover consciousness, so I can interview him. I'll keep you informed. I really want to share dinner with you and Shaun tonight. This is an important occasion, celebrating being in your new home." He punched the off button, wishing she had been available to talk.

Questions plagued him the whole way to the hospital. Had whoever impersonated Dawson attacked Tom? Why? Where was the guy now, and what was he after?

* * *

"Don't answer it." Imposter held his hand out. "Give me your cell phone. As soon as I get what I've come for, I'll leave. Police will only mess everything up. I'll be forced to do something I don't want to do."

Seated next to Shaun on the couch, Lacey wished she could have talked with Ryan. Imposter—no, she was going to call him Trey as she had for the past weeks—

snatched her phone from her grasp. As long as she had it, she'd felt a connection to Ryan. She'd hoped to have a chance to alert Ryan about what was happening. She needed to find another way. When he came to dinner, he'd be held captive or worse, and end up like the real Trey Dawson.

"Trust me. I'll be gone soon."

Through the last five minutes, Sadie hadn't barked once. Had this man done something to her? The dog was in her kennel and wouldn't have been able to attack Trey. Maybe she was quiet because the painter was familiar to her. "Sadie has been in her crate for a few hours. I need to give her some water. You can watch and make sure that's all."

"No need. I gave her something to sleep."

Shaun gasped.

Trey turned his attention to Shaun. "Come over here."

Her son's eyes grew huge.

"Now!"

Shaun flinched but slowly moved toward Trey.

"Turn around." After Shaun did, Trey grabbed a length of rope. "Put your hands behind your back."

He didn't.

Trey jerked first one arm then the other behind Shaun and wound the rope around his wrists.

Tears ran down Shaun's face.

Lacey rose a few inches off the couch.

"Sit!" Trey shifted his focus to her, his look menacing, like daggers stabbing her. "You're next. If you follow my directions, you'll be okay."

Like the real Trey Dawson was. She couldn't believe a word this man said. The only one she could trust was the Lord. He would give her a way out of here unharmed.

Trey had her son sit next to her. Then he motioned for her to stand. While he tied her hands behind her, he asked, "What's your security code?"

She told him, and when she settled next to Shaun, he walked to the security pad by the door and set it to go off if anyone left the carriage house. The very device used to keep people out would keep them in.

He came back into the living area. "This way I can work freely without worrying you're gonna escape. The quicker I find the dia—what I came for, the quicker I'll be gone." He took another piece of rope and tied her feet then started to do Shaun's too, but her son sobbed against Lacey's side. Trey stuffed the rope in his pocket. "Stay put and this will be over soon."

As he left, Lacey said, "Thank you."

Trey paused in the entrance into her bedroom. "For what?"

"For not scaring my son anymore."

He gave her an odd look right before he disappeared into the room.

She was furious with the man, but she'd meant the thank you. "Shaun, we might not have a lot of time to talk freely."

Her son twisted toward her, blinking his red eyes.

"Turn your back to me and let me try to untie your hands," she whispered. "If I can, then you can go into your closet and escape through the trap door. Use the stepladder I left in there."

"But—" he said in his normal voice.

"Shh," she said over the banging and sawing noise coming from her room.

"How do I get out of the attic?"

"This is the only time I want you to do this. Jump to the tree branch and climb down. Get to the house and have them call Ryan. He and the Bells will know what to do." She would never have suggested that to Shaun, but she needed him totally safe. The limb was only inches away and would hold his weight.

"But you'll be in here. He'll hurt you. Like he did Sadie." His voice caught on his dog's name.

"Hon, Sadie will be all right. He said he gave her something to sleep." Lacey had to believe the man was telling the truth. If Sadie was dead, Shaun would be devastated. So would she. "Shaun, he isn't going to hurt me. He'll use me as a hostage so he can get away once he finds the diamonds. I don't want you involved. I have to know you're safe. Can you do it?"

He nodded and shifted so he faced

away from her. While she turned and worked on his ropes, she kept an eye on the doorway into her bedroom. She heard shuffling of feet and whispered, "Sit back."

Trey poked his head through the entrance. He didn't say anything but returned to his work.

After she resumed loosening his knots, she inhaled to keep herself calm and said, "Let's hurry. He was gone about fifteen minutes, so I need you out of here and safe before he comes and checks again."

Five minutes later Shaun jumped to his feet, hands untied. "I'll do yours."

"No. Go. You don't have much time." The sound of Trey destroying what had just been renovated should have angered her, but right now as long as it went on, her son would be safe.

At the door into his bedroom, he hesitated and glanced back.

She nodded her head and mouthed the word, "Go."

Now the waiting began. Probably no more than ten minutes before Trey would be back to check on them.

* * *

Ryan stood at the side of Tom's bed at the hospital. "I'm glad you'll be all right. Having suffered a concussion recently, I can tell you that you should be much better in a week or so. I only have a few questions. Then one of my deputies will take your statement later. Do you know who did this to you?"

"Trey Dawson. I came into my office and found him going through my files on my computer. Some papers he'd filled out were on the desk by him. Before I could react, he was out of my chair and came at me. The next thing I remember is being transported to the hospital by the paramedics."

"What kind of papers?"

"His employment information, current address, as well as a contact number. Why would he take that?"

"Because he isn't the real Trey Dawson. He was covering his tracks. Do you remember where he was staying?"

"At the Sunflower Motel."

"Thanks. I'll check in later to see how you're doing." He walked toward the door.

"What's going on?"

Ryan paused before leaving. "I'm not sure, but the fake Dawson most likely murdered the real one."

Tom's jaw dropped. "I guess I'm lucky to be alive."

Ryan spoke to Deputy Carter outside Tom's room. "Stay here and watch him. Don't let anyone but staff or family in there. When he's up to it, take a statement of the events. He might remember more later."

"Where are you going, Sheriff?"

"To catch a killer."

Ryan couldn't shake the urgency that took hold of him and squeezed. When he reached the Sunflower Motel, he found the assailant was gone. He hadn't paid his bill or checked out, but there was nothing in his room. It hadn't been cleaned yet, so he had Deputy Washburn process the area for fingerprints.

Standing outside by his SUV, he called Lacey. It again went to voicemail. He kneaded his shoulder and neck. His gut roiled with tension. Something wasn't right.

* * *

Lacey looked at the clock on her kitchen wall. Ten minutes since Shaun left. Had he made it? Was he safe now with Harriet and Richard? She'd asked a lot of her son, but with him gone at least she could breathe easier. Sweat ran down her face as she imagined all the possibilities.

Suddenly she stopped. Live in the moment. Don't worry about what could be.

He's in Your hands, Lord. He's safe.

Again silence from the other room, then the sound of footsteps growing closer. She closed her eyes and fortified herself with a vision of Shaun free, smiling, safe.

"Where's your son?"

She shrugged. "I untied his hands, gave him the code, and told him to leave."

Trey stormed toward the security pad. "It's still on. Is he hiding in here?"

She didn't say anything.

Trey crossed the room, jerked her to

her feet, and wrapped his hands around her neck. Then he squeezed.

* * *

Ryan drove toward his house, pushing the speed limit. Pain streaked across his shoulders and down his neck and spine. Every muscle in his body tightened into a hard knot. He needed to see Lacey. Then he'd laugh about his frantic drive to the bed and breakfast.

He called her again. Nothing. He started to punch in Richard's number when his cell phone rang. He quickly answered without looking at who it was and automatically said, "Lacey."

"No, this is Harriet. Shaun is here in the house. He's shaking and saying that the painter has his mother. Then something about jumping to a tree and climbing down."

"Lock the doors. Don't open them except for me. I'm two minutes away. The painter who worked at the B and B killed a man. Calm Shaun down. I need to know how he got out of the carriage house."

He disconnected from the call and floored the gas pedal. If he'd been there when he said he would be, maybe he could have prevented this. A minute later, he pounded on the front door.

Richard, holding a rolling pin, opened the door. "What took you so long? We're upstairs where we can keep an eye on the carriage house."

At the window in the Harbor Suite on the second floor, Ryan stared down at the building where Lacey was being held. "How did you get out without the painter knowing?" he asked Shaun.

"Mom told me to use the trap door in my closet. It leads to the attic. Then I jumped to a branch on the big oak tree out back by the double doors."

Ryan pictured that part of the carriage house and sucked in a deep breath. That was a fourteen-foot drop. The situation was bad if Lacey told him to do that. "Why is he there?"

"Mom says looking for diamonds."

"Diamonds!" Harriet exclaimed. "Where

did she get that idea?"

"From that man." Tears filled Shaun's eyes. "Please save her. I can show you how I got out."

Ryan knelt in front of Shaun and clasped his arms. "I will. Don't worry. You stay here with Harriet and Richard."

Shaun swiped the wet rivulets from his cheeks and nodded.

Richard followed Ryan into the hall.

"Call the station and tell them about the hostage situation. Until they hear from me, I don't want their presence known to anyone in the carriage house, so they need to take cover."

"Will do."

* * *

Lacey's throat burned, the pressure around her neck making her lightheaded. "I'm not good to you dead," she managed to squeak out.

He squeezed tighter.

His face spun before her eyes, and she closed them.

Suddenly he released her and shoved her onto the couch. "You'd better hope I find the diamonds soon. If I can't escape, you'll die. I have nothing to lose now. I hope the sheriff cares about you and he'll back off when we leave."

"We?"

"Yeah, you'll go with me until I feel safe and free. Then I might let you go."

Might?

Don't panic. A lot can happen. God is with me.

"You're coming with me." He stared down at her tied feet, bent over, and scooped her up into his arms.

Bile clogged her throat.

He dropped her onto her bed. "Don't move an inch." The glare that accompanied the implied threat bore into her.

She nodded.

* * *

Ryan stared up at the open double doors above him. With a ladder from his garage, he'd sneaked up to the carriage house and propped it against the building. It wasn't quite tall enough for him to easily crawl into the attic. He would have to haul himself up to the opening.

He scrambled up the ladder. Every second counted. Once the fake Dawson discovered Shaun was gone, no telling what the man would do. At the top, he perched on tiptoes, got a good grip of the ledge, then hoisted himself into the attic. Breathing hard, he hurried across the floor to where Shaun's room should be and spied the trap door.

He withdrew his gun and crept down the steps into Shaun's closet. The light was on, but the door was closed. Smart thinking on Shaun's part.

A string of curses wafted to him. The killer was losing it, getting angry. Not a good sign. Ryan eased the door open. As he sneaked out of the closet and across Shaun's bedroom, something like a sledgehammer struck against the wall. The sound urged him to move faster. Out in the hallway, he sidled up to the entrance to Lacey's room and slowly peered through the crack created by the open door. He caught sight of Lacey on her bed.

Their gazes met, and she gave him a smile.

"Why do you think it's in here?" Lacey asked in a hoarse voice.

"Because I didn't search this part of the house much the first time. It has to be here. I'll find it if I have to tear down all the walls." Frustration and anger coated each of the fake Dawson's words.

"How do you know there are diamonds stashed here?"

What had the killer done to Lacey to make her voice so raspy? Ryan fought the rage threatening to rob him of his control.

"My cellmate told me they were hidden in a crevice in the carriage house."

"Where did the diamonds come from?"

"He robbed a big jewelry company outside D.C. nineteen years ago. He got caught not long after he hid them here."

"Crevice doesn't necessarily mean the wall. What if it's under the floorboards— under the carpet. When I was a little girl and played in here, there were some loose planks that I used to hide things in."

The killer came into view through the crack. He clutched a sledgehammer. Ryan aimed his gun through the opening.

"Where?"

"Living area, not far from the large bay window."

Dawson bent over and untied the ropes around her ankles. "Get up. Show me." He moved out of Ryan's view. "Hurry."

"I'm moving as fast as I can." She swung her legs off the bed and then stood.

Ryan flattened himself against the wall and waited.

When Lacey left her bedroom, her gaze cut toward him although her head only moved slightly. Ryan tensed, preparing himself for the confrontation. As he caught a glimpse of the killer holding the sledgehammer, Lacey dodged to the side as though she were going to run toward the front door. Her captor surged forward, his attention on her.

That gave Ryan the edge he needed. He raised his gun. "Stop or I'll shoot."

The guy swung around, the

Margaret Daley

sledgehammer gripped in both of his hands as if it were a shield. "No, you won't. I'm unarmed."

Ryan laughed humorlessly. "Wrong. A sledgehammer can kill. If I feel threatened or Lacey does, then I have a right to protect her or myself. So come at me and test whether I'll shoot or not."

When the killer raised his weapon, Lacey charged into his back, sending him flying to the floor.

Ryan moved quickly. He yanked the sledgehammer from the fake Dawson and shoved the gun into the man's back. "At this range, I guarantee I won't miss."

The fake Dawson went slack.

As Ryan put handcuffs on him, he glanced at Lacey. "Okay?"

"Yes, I am now."

Once the prisoner was secured, Ryan moved to Lacey and loosened the ropes around her wrists then helped her to her feet. He scooped her into his arms and hugged her tight. He didn't want to let go, but he needed to notify his deputies the hostage was safe.

174

* * *

Lacey sat in the living room of the bed and breakfast, holding Shaun against her. She didn't want to let him go. What he did today had saved her. The killer would have had no reason to keep her alive after he escaped the carriage house. She'd seen it in his cold eyes.

"Shaun, we can sleep in the Garden Suite tonight."

Her son didn't say anything.

She leaned forward and realized Shaun had fallen asleep with Sadie cuddled next to him. No wonder he hadn't said anything for the last five minutes. She moved slowly and laid his head gently on the cushion. When she stood and stared at him, tears glistened in her eyes. She could have lost him today. She could...

Stop the what ifs. Cherish what's happening right at this moment. Peace settled on her shoulders as she gazed on her son, then she looked at the living room of her bed and breakfast thanks to Mr. Hopewell. She had been blessed today.

Thank You, Lord.

"The carriage house has been processed."

Ryan's words, so sweet to her ears, bathed her in warmth. When he had hugged her after subduing the killer, she'd felt cherished and hopeful for the future. She'd never thought she would allow herself to love again, but Sheriff Ryan McNeil had stolen her heart, probably from the very first day she arrived back home after almost twenty years.

He stood right behind her. She faced him and wound her arms around him. "We're going to stay in the Garden Suite one more day."

He led her to the loveseat, catty-corner from the couch and sat, tugging her down next to him. "I'm taking most of tomorrow off. I'll help you fix the damage he did to your bedroom."

"Did you find the diamonds?" There had been a couple of places she'd thought might be where the gems were hidden that hadn't been searched yet. She'd told Ryan about them and hoped he could find the diamonds.

He nodded. "At the far end of the attic where the double doors are, between the outside wall and the garage below. After I spied a black bag, two of my deputies went into the garage and knocked a hole in the wall behind the shelving. Millions of dollars in diamonds were inside. After nineteen years, they'll be returned to their rightful owner—Collins Diamond Emporium." Ryan cuddled her against him. "I'm seizing the moment. I'm not letting anymore time pass without telling you that I love you. I hope one day we can be a family—you, me, and Shaun."

His words took her breath away.

"Will you marry me, Lacey St. John?"

"Mom, tell him yes." Sitting up on the couch, Shaun rubbed his eyes.

"Yeah, Lacey, tell me yes." Smiling at her, Ryan winked.

"Yes. I love you." She threw her arms around his neck. "My sister is going to be so jealous. You were all she talked about when we moved away."

"Yay! Mom's gonna marry Ryan." Her

sleepy son was suddenly wide awake.

Sadie barked her approval.

"I second that, Shaun. Yay!" Ryan wrapped his arms around Lacey and kissed her.

Thanks, Mr. Hopewell, for this second chance at love.

—The End—

DEADLY HUNT

Book 1 in
Strong Women, Extraordinary Situations
by Margaret Daley

All bodyguard Tess Miller wants is a vacation. But when a wounded stranger stumbles into her isolated cabin in the Arizona mountains, Tess becomes his lifeline. When Shane Burkhart opens his eyes, all he can focus on is his guardian angel leaning over him. And in the days to come he will need a guardian angel while being hunted by someone who wants him dead.

DEADLY INTENT

Book 2 in
Strong Women, Extraordinary Situations
by Margaret Daley

Texas Ranger Sarah Osborn thought she would never see her high school sweetheart, Ian O'Leary, again. But fifteen years later, Ian, an ex-FBI agent, has someone targeting him, and she's assigned to the case. Can Sarah protect Ian and her heart?

DEADLY HOLIDAY

Book 3 in
Strong Women, Extraordinary Situations
by Margaret Daley

Tory Caldwell witnesses a hit-and-run, but when the dead victim disappears from the scene, police doubt a crime has been committed. Tory is threatened when she keeps insisting she saw a man killed and the only one who believes her is her neighbor, Jordan Steele. Together, can they solve the mystery of the disappearing body and stay alive?

DEADLY COUNTDOWN

Book Four in
Strong Women, Extraordinary Situations
by Margaret Daley

Allie Martin, a widow, has a secret protector who manipulates her life without anyone knowing until…

When Remy Broussard, an injured police officer, returns to Port David, Louisiana to visit before his medical leave is over, he discovers his childhood friend, Allie Martin, is being stalked. As Remy protects Allie and tries to find her stalker, they realize their feelings go beyond friendship.

When the stalker is found, they begin to explore the deeper feelings they have for each other, only to have a more sinister threat come between them. Will Allie be able to save Remy before he dies at the hand of a maniac?

DEADLY NOEL

Book Five in
Strong Women, Extraordinary Situations
by Margaret Daley

Assistant DA, Kira Davis, convicted the wrong man—Gabriel Michaels, a single dad with a young daughter. When new evidence was brought forth, his conviction was overturned, and Gabriel returned home to his ranch to put his life back together. Although Gabriel is free, the murderer of his wife is still out there and resumes killing women. In a desperate alliance, Kira and Gabriel join forces to find the true identity of the person terrorizing their town. Will they be able to forgive the past and find the killer before it's too late?

DEADLY DOSE

Book Six in
Strong Women, Extraordinary Situations
by Margaret Daley

When Jessie Michaels discovers a letter written to her by her deceased best friend, she is determined to find who murdered Mary Lou, at first thought to be a victim of a serial killer by the police. Jessie's questions lead to an attempt on her life. The last man she wanted to come to her aid was Josh Morgan, the wealthy businessman who had been instrumental in her brother going to prison. Together they uncover a drug ring that puts them both in danger. Will Jessie and Josh find the killer? Love? Or will one of them fall victim to a DEADLY DOSE?

About the Author

USA Today Bestselling author, Margaret Daley, is multi-published with over 95 titles and 5 million books sold worldwide. She had written for Harlequin, Abingdon, Kensington, Dell, and Simon and Schuster. She has won multiple awards, including the prestigious Carol Award, Holt Medallion and Inspirational Readers' Choice Contest.

She has been married for over forty years and has a son and two granddaughters. When she isn't traveling, she's writing love stories, often with a suspense thread and corralling her three cats that think they rule her household.

To find out more about Margaret visit her website at www.margaretdaley.com.

Made in the USA
San Bernardino, CA
14 January 2020